Bait 4 a Trap

Ann Stang

Thank you:

My husband and children for your love and encouragement and for reading my stuff, over and over and over.

Kim Todd and my daughter Kelli for your valuable suggestions and editing.

My son and my daughter-in-law, David and Rebekah. I wouldn't have done this for a long, long time without your help publishing, including the perfect cover that is just as I envisioned it, Rebekah.

My parents for your love and support in everything I've done. Mom, I wish I could have shared this with you.

May this, as always, be for the glory of God.

Prologue

"America's Attic,'" muttered U.S. Senator Lloyd Sinclair to himself, looking around the Smithsonian. "This exhibit should be named 'Stranded in the 50s.'" He was in the middle of an exhibit at the museum showing life circa 1950, including a happy homemaker ironing away as if her life depended on it. She was dressed as if she was about to go out for a night on the town with her equally perky husband who, dressed in a conservative business suit and carrying a briefcase must have just come home from the office. Sinclair wanted to loosen his tie, just so he wouldn't look like he was part of the annoying exhibit. He turned his back on it.

"Stuck in the exhibit is more like it," he scowled. He'd been told to meet his contact there. No doubt because it would be deserted. Senator Sinclair looked at his watch and tapped an envelope against his leg. A young woman in a ponytail corralled her two small children quickly past the exhibit, barely giving it or him a glance. He felt the same about the exhibit, but didn't he merit even a look? He couldn't get used to being invisible. He blamed it on aging. It was obvious women no longer found him attractive. He ran his hand over his balding head. Life was so unfair. Women should have to be bald, he thought. He looked down at his ever-increasing waistline. That might have something to do with it, too, he admitted. He loosened his tie.

His contact was almost fifteen minutes late. He

stretched and pulled out his phone to see if they'd messaged. No text. How long was he expected to wait here?

An announcement came over the loudspeaker as if in answer to his unspoken question. "The Smithsonian will be closing in fifteen minutes. Please use this time to phone for a ride home if you need it."

"Closing? This is a crazy place to meet. Why am I here?" he whispered.

A sudden thought occurred to him. He broke out in a cold sweat and felt the heart palpitations he dreaded. Why *was* he here? Of all of the places they could have chosen in Washington, D.C., why here? He hadn't requested this rendezvous spot. Why hadn't he questioned it before? Of course, he was the one who wanted no paper trail to lead to him, so he wasn't willing to access the money electronically. Wiping clammy hands on his trousers, he looked at his watch again. Hearing a noise behind him, he turned toward the next exhibit. He didn't see anyone, but he felt eyes on him. The exhibits were well lit, but the spaces between were full of shadows. He shook his head.

"Don't let your imagination run away with you," he muttered to himself angrily.

A short, pudgy man approached from the other direction. This had to be him. Sinclair took a deep breath. Finally. The palpitations continued. He pressed on his chest for a second before dropping his hand to approach the man.

"I deal in facts and figures, not clandestine meetings. Why did the DNC arrange to meet here?"

The man wasn't buying the brusqueness. "You know why. Just give it to me."

Sinclair hesitated. This was his last chance to walk away, last chance before giving his ambition full reign.

"Don't you have something for me?" he said quietly looking over his shoulder to see if anyone was listening.

"First the Social Security fraud info."

Sinclair wanted to clamp his hand over the man's mouth. He looked around furtively, but there was still no one around. The senator passed him the envelope.

"Your position on the Senate Committee on Finance certainly was lucrative for you, wasn't it?" The man sneered.

In his younger days, Sinclair would have buttoned the lip of anyone who talked to him snidely. Today all he wanted was to get his money and get out of there.

"Just give me my fee."

"Fee... Ha! That's a good one."

"Give me the money," Sinclair said.

"Not so fast." The man was looking over the information. Sinclair pulled out a handkerchief and wiped his forehead. "I was told to make sure we aren't blackmailed twice."

"Blackmail is such an ugly word. I prefer to think of it as mutually beneficial to both the party and to me."

Another announcement came over the speaker. "We will be closing in 10 minutes." The woman sounded bored.

"This is the only copy?" The man stared unblinking at the senator.

"No honor among thieves?" he joked. The other man didn't smile. "Of course it's the only copy." *With me,* Sinclair finished the thought in his head.

The man handed Sinclair a bulging #10 envelope. Such a small package, yet it held the answer to all of his dreams. He started to count the money.

The man laughed. Sinclair looked up from his counting.

"America's Attic!" the man chuckled.

"Most boring exhibit in the place. I suppose that's why they picked it... no people around." Sinclair resumed counting.

"And because there are no cameras," the man said quietly as he walked away.

Before he was out of sight, a tall, rugged man came from behind the placard of a nearby exhibit. Sinclair froze, the stealthy tread behind him registering too late amid the numbers in his head. Sinclair turned, barely evading the short blade of the knife as the man lunged at him.

Sinclair took off in a gait that for him was running. He'd run track in high school, but that was several decades and more than 50 pounds ago. As he ran, the lights overhead flicked on and off. The place was closing! He had to get to the exit before the Smithsonian closed down for the night. He could feel his heart racing, and his breath came in gasps. As he dodged in and out of exhibits, the pain in his side made it hurt to breathe.

He couldn't do it, couldn't run anymore. Sinclair looked around for a weapon. Panting, he grabbed a sword from a medieval knight exhibit, but it was bolted down. He cursed, broke off a piece of a ceramic dragon's tail, and turned to defend himself. The attacker knocked the makeshift weapon out of his hand as though combating a child. He plunged his knife into the senator's stomach, but the angle sliced through only visceral fat. He pulled it out and raised it to strike again. As the senator cast about for something else to use as a weapon, the attacker plunged his knife into the senator's back. Sinclair collapsed against the heavy knight, pulling it down on him with a clatter. The attacker pried the envelope of money from Sinclair's hands, pulled him behind a nearby display, and left.

Sinclair came to. He couldn't move into the main walkway, but he managed to push the knight off himself enough to reach his cell phone. He knew he had one chance before he passed out. He could barely press the buttons. The Smithsonian would be closing any second. He couldn't count on someone coming by in time to save him.

As he started to press 9-1-1, the attacker came running back, yanked the phone out of his hand, and started away. The senator tried to yell, but only a whisper came out, "Wait, please, I've got more mon-" but his attacker ignored him, running faster down the hall as another announcement came over the speaker.

"The Smithsonian is now closed. Please be

advised: this   is   your   last   call."

One

Over the beeping of the alarm clock, Madison McPherson said in her best Grinchy voice, "I must stop morning from coming, but how?" Where did that reference come from on this warm summer day?

She eyed the alarm, considering. She could hit snooze a few times but knew she'd regret it if she did. Off went the alarm clock.

Maddie rolled over and stared at the ceiling, but a reminder to get up met her gaze as her alarm clock shone the time of day on the ceiling. She tried to will herself to get up, but her pep talk came out sounding more like regret. "Note to self: three grande Starbucks iced coffees in the evening wasn't a good idea. Not if I wanted to get any sleep last night." She rolled over and nudged Franky, her longhaired miniature dachshund, who continued to breathe softly and evenly. "Franky, it's time to get up." The dog inched away from her and went back to sleep.

Leaving the rumpled covers to make later after Frank got up, she wrestled free, pulled on her cushy pink robe and matching bunny slippers, and headed to the kitchen for the most important part of her day.

Bleary-eyed and almost disoriented in her kitchen, Maddie tried to remember why everything was out of place. Where was her coffeemaker? It took a full fifteen seconds for her to remember she had decided it was more efficient for the appliance to be next to the sink. It was hiding behind her giant lighthouse cookie jar. Maddie sighed. Was it going to be one of those days?

Putting on a pot of coffee, she grabbed her Bible and stepped out onto the small balcony to get some light, "in more ways than one," she mused to herself smiling.

From this vantage point, she could see the neighbor's cat, Snowball, was sneaking up on a cardinal. Step by step, Snowball crept until he was just about within pouncing distance. Maddie reached through the railing around her balcony to pull out of the gutter a few sticks that must have dropped from the tree after the last storm. A couple of well-aimed tosses at Snowball caused the cat to move, giving away his position, and the bird flew safely away.

"My good deed for the day," Maddie crowed. "You'll just have to be content with cat chow," she called to the feline gleefully. Snowball looked up at her when she spoke, and Maddie swore the cat scowled before he disappeared into a stand of trees.

One glance at the gathering clouds warned her she might soon have to cancel her plans to enjoy her morning outside. Picking up in the book of Mark where she had left off the day before, Maddie sank into her chaise lounge. She read about the three women bringing spices to anoint the body of Jesus. "And they said among themselves, 'Who will roll away the stone from the door of the tomb for us?'" she read aloud, wondering how none of the people who knew Jesus so well understood at all what He was doing. "How could they be so blind? They lived with Him, listened to the things He said, and still didn't understand that He was the Son of God."

Maddie looked around at the quiet yard and pictured herself on the way to the tomb. "Who will roll away the stone from the door of the tomb for us?" she repeated. Had she encountered things in life as large, figuratively, as a boulder that she didn't have the strength to move?

Her father's face replaced the image of the stone. Was anything more immovable than her father once he had his mind set on an idea?

The last thing she wanted to think about was their strained father-daughter relationship. The promised rain started to scatter across her small balcony and brought her out of her musing. The young, red maple tree that gave any shade threw its shadows only when she sat out here in the evening. Its sparse foliage wasn't giving any refuge from the thickening rain. Maddie picked up her Bible and rushed inside just as it started to pour. Too late, she realized she'd forgotten her coffee. She stood looking through the French doors as her mug filled with rain and overflowed.

Journalist Jay Clark reached for the speech transcription resting on his dining room table. Bitingly he read aloud for the umpteenth time from the much-handled pages." And just as Ronald Reagan said, 'Freedom is never more than one generation from extinction. We didn't pass it to our children in the bloodstream. It must be fought for,

protected, and handed on to them to do the same.'"
He tossed the pages on the table in disgust. They
glided smoothly across the glass top and came to
rest teetering on the edge for a second before
sliding off onto the carpet. An extremely large
German shepherd walked soundlessly over and
nosed the stack of papers.

"No, Riley. Leave it alone. Even you wouldn't
eat that drivel." Jay picked up the pages again
considering and shook his head thinking drivel
wasn't an accurate term. It was well written.
Coming out of anyone else's mouth, it could have
been eloquent, but it just didn't ring true when the
Dishonorable Senator Dalton Q. Stanfield gave this
speech. It was as if he were lip-synching for the real
artist. How dare he quote a conservative as if he
agreed with him!

Jay sat down again at his dining room table.
He liked to have all of his notes spread around him
and plenty of room to work. He read the short
speech again. Riley crawled under the dining room
table and rested his head on Jay's feet. Jay reached
down to pet the dog and noticed he had a callous
on his hand from his last workout. Maybe he'd
been overdoing it lately. Riley vigorously licked the
callous.

Jay barely noticed. The phrase "fought for,
protected" had inspired him. Fighting for freedom
was the reason he got out of bed in the morning,
only he used his column rather than a gun to
protect the people of the nation from the duplicity
of its leaders. He knew what direction this column
would go. He pulled his hand back and bent over

his work. Riley sighed and rested his head on his paws.

Turning from the ruined coffee and the pouring rain, Maddie surveyed her apartment. Small by most standards, she'd always referred to it as cozy. It was the upstairs of a story-and-a-half stone cottage, quaint and covered with ivy. All of her ceilings sloped rather steeply, but since she was short, she could still stand up in most places. She'd decorated with garage sale finds, preferring that route to digging further into debt. That master's degree didn't come cheap. There was a bit of a sea-faring theme, just enough to reflect her love of the coast, but not enough to be obnoxious. She looked around now as the storm darkened the room.

"A nor'easter, she be blowing in," she said ominously to Franky who had joined her. He rolled over on his back and snored softly. "Okay, maybe not, but it could be."

Maddie blew some dust from her shelf, heavy with books she meant to read. She remembered thinking in college that as soon as she was done with school and didn't have a required reading list, she would catch up within a week on the stack of books she wanted to read. Well, there they sat. She rearranged a couple of them and made a mental note to start reading before bed.

Maddie's exercise bike nagged her from the corner. Her purse dangled from the handlebars, and she could see she'd have to dust before she could use it. She turned on a few lamps, set some pillows back in their places on the couch, and looked around. "It's no castle, but it's warm and dry and cozy." The rivulets of water running down the outside of the window in the grey light only accented how safe and warm she felt to be inside. She nodded in approval. At least the roof didn't leak. It was time to get to work.

Maddie had started her first real job a few months ago, speechwriter for a United States senator. It had been her dream to do this since she'd studied the speeches of President Reagan. They had helped change the course of history, especially "Tear down this wall, Mr. Gorbechav."

Even though she would type it out eventually, Maddie always planned them on index cards first. As she arranged the cards in neat rows, she pushed her glasses up with one finger on the arm giving herself a lop-sided look and began reading what she'd written the night before. "Wow, was I wired - way too much coffee. What did I have the senator call himself... a Neo-conservative?" She crossed out the sentence and smiled, thinking of Senator Dalton Stanfield, her boss. Not only was he good-looking, but also he was such an intellectual. "And he has integrity," she reminded herself, "which is the quality I admire most about him."

Maddie looked around for her coffee mug; then she remembered it was on the balcony, now filled with rainwater. She poured herself another cup, added a generous amount of cream, and padded back to the living room. She carefully placed the cup on its coaster on the coffee table and straightened her index cards again. "Time to get started." Maddie headed to the bedroom to get her new laptop. She smiled and stretched. It was so relaxing to work in her pajamas.

Republican Senator Dalton Stanfield entered the Hart Senate Office Building as he had so many mornings, fully aware of his importance. He smoothed his sleek, black hair with just a touch of silver at the temples as he looked around to see who was there. News crews often shot footage in the bright, soaring lobby. Today though, there was nobody, just tourists, an irritating, but a necessary evil.

He stopped to read the inscription describing Senator Hart after whom the building was named, not sure why it caught his eye today. He'd almost ceased to notice it although the inscription had inspired him as a young senator. "A man of incorruptible integrity and personal courage strengthened by inner grace and outer gentleness... He advanced the cause of human justice, promoted the welfare of the common man, and improved the quality of life... His humility and ethics earned him his place as the conscience of the Senate."

Dalton paused and stared for a moment at the words, thinking back even earlier, to his days as a state representative. He'd gotten into politics to help his country, to help his fellow man. What had happened to the young idealist? Dalton grunted. He'd learned the only way to do anything, the only way to help people was to play the game. That was what had happened to him.

Dalton brushed aside the prick to his conscience that the quote caused and continued through the atrium. The idealist who had read those words, who had wanted to emulate Senator Hart was gone and a realist had taken his place. The career that had begun with a sincere desire to help his constituents was becoming a high-powered game to Dalton. A game he intended to win. His ambitions trumped everything else, and he felt few qualms about it now, rationalizing that he could help more people as his career advanced. "We all win then."

Approaching the enormous sculpture *Mountains and Clouds*, he walked around it rather than through it. It was large enough to pass through, to become for a time a living part of the famous sculpture. But such flights of fancy were for tourists. He had ceased to be awed.

His lavish suite of offices was nearly empty now since Congress wasn't in session. Entering his administrative assistant Jeanie's office, he was surprised to find her already at work typing a letter given to her yesterday. She rarely beat him to the office.

"Good morning, Senator," Jeanie smiled and returned to her work.

"Good morning, Jeanie. You're here uncharacteristically early."

"I'm on time, sir," she said, puzzled.

"That's what I said," Dalton continued into his office and shut the door. He laid his computer on his table and sat behind his desk. Rifling through a stack of papers, he sighed. The woman's filing system was known only to her. He pressed the intercom button to summon Jeanie. She knocked and entered his office after a few minutes, long enough for Dalton to become impatient, but he was often impatient with her.

"Jeanie, I need that file that I asked you to have ready for me first thing this morning."

She winced. "Oh, I'm so sorry, Senator. I forgot. I'll get right to work on it."

Dalton drew in a deep breath. "That's fine, Jeanie. Just get started on it." Jeanie quickly left his office, and Dalton moved to his computer. Jeanie had no idea what his real work was, and that was the way he wanted it. Her naiveté was a good cover for his operations. Few in Washington realized he'd started his career as a Democrat.

Advancing his career was his focus now, not some pie-in-the-sky ideals. The quote was completely forgotten.

Tiffany Roberts turned, examining herself from every angle in her three-way mirror. Not a wrinkle in the fabric, not a hair out of place, her morning routine was done. Her mother had taught her to look herself over completely, and then go out into the world with confidence. Her long, shiny black hair seemed to have a life of its own but always returned to its original spot without assistance. Satisfied with her appearance, she moved into the kitchen to prepare her morning latte.

Ebony followed her leaving behind her favorite mouse toy that Tiffany had bought to exercise the cat. It had a timer to move spontaneously every few minutes, and so far it still fooled the feline. Ebony jumped onto the counter, slinked over to the espresso machine, and watched as Tiffany brewed coffee. When Tiffany got the bottle of milk out of the refrigerator, Ebony crept closer. Tiffany poured a small amount of milk into a bowl and set it on the floor, luring the cat away from the latte preparations. Lately, the cat had taken to swiping at the milk as it foamed, once even dipping her paw into the small pitcher. No one got between Tiffany and her first cup of coffee, not even her beloved Ebony, so the feline had to be content to lap up the cold milk set on the floor after that.

Tiffany foamed the milk and poured it expertly into the cup. She'd worked as a barista while in college and ever after disdained anything less than gourmet coffee.

She carried her cup to the art deco kitchen table and sat down, scooting in closer as Ebony made a move to jump onto her lap. "You know better than that," she reprimanded the cat as she opened her laptop. "I can't have cat hair on my dress." Ebony leaped onto another chair and then onto the table, carefully padding over to situate herself next to the latte. The cat watched intently, her flicking tail the only sign she was alive, but Tiffany never took her hand off the cup.

Tiffany checked her favorite sites to see what was happening in D.C. since she'd retired the night before. Keeping up on the pulse of the heartbeat of the nation, as she saw her city, occupied her every waking moment. She had no time or patience for hobbies. She intended to move up from her job as a U.S. senator's aide quickly.

Politics were in her DNA. Her great-grandfather Franklin Roberts had been a governor. He had always worked behind the scenes in the Democrat party; a "wheeler-dealer" her father had often called him, usually in a thinly veiled sarcastic tone. Early on Tiffany's father had rebelled against Grandpa Roberts and the political system, even refusing to vote. He eschewed big-city living, assuming the desire for luxury was the reason behind his father's way of life, moving during Tiffany's early years to the wide-open spaces of rural eastern Washington state.

But Tiffany knew it was more than a luxurious lifestyle her grandfather craved. It was the power. The kind of power her grandfather had was like a hot air balloon. It had the capability of rising high above everything else and taking you with it, but only if you were willing to turn up the heat. The hotter you cranked it, the higher you flew. Tiffany intended to fly very high.

As she sipped her latte, she reviewed the plan she would set in motion that day. She had accessed confidential information that she would sell. It should garner her quite a bit of money. Of course, money wasn't her only goal, but she would need it to move ahead in her career. Her mother's words echoed in her mind, "You can work hard, or you can work smart." Tiffany was very smart.

She stroked Ebony, who relaxed and purred beneath her hand. They were alike in a way, focused. All Tiffany needed was the right mouse.

Two

Maddie noticed Frank was no longer in the bedroom and called out to him, "Frank, where are you?" She heard a noise in the living room and assumed he'd decided to join her in there.

Her phone rang while she was getting her laptop. It was her sister, and Maddie considered not answering it. "If I get sidetracked now, I'll never get this done in time, and Dalton needs this today." She always thought of him as Dalton now, rather than Senator Stanfield as she had called him when she started as his speechwriter three months ago. "Dalton needs time to practice this before he makes his appearance at the dedication of the new building at the university tomorrow."

She plopped down on the bed and answered her phone. Hearing noise started already in the background, she would have known who it was without looking at the name displayed on the screen. Her sister always had on music or the news.

Explaining the need to get back to work, Maddie tried to cut the conversation short, which didn't sit well with Lizette who complained, "How come you never have time for me anymore? I swear you work more hours than I do." As a nurse, Lizette was very dedicated to her job, so Maddie brushed off the criticism lightly. "Liz, you know I love my job, and I want to do well since this is my first writing job. The only way to get ahead is to jump in and grab the bull by the horns. Whatever that means."

"You sound like Dad. He always says 'grab the bull by the horns.' Have you talked to him lately?"

"Not lately," Maddie hedged.

"Not at all, you mean. He's your father. He loves you, you know."

"Even though I am a huge disappointment to him? Anyway, I called Mom last week."

"But you didn't talk to Dad, did you?"

After a pause, Maddie said, "She can relay my news to him."

"Hearing things secondhand is not a relationship. I just don't want you to regret all of this someday." Once again, Maddie felt sympathy for her brother-in-law, Noah, who was now the designated recipient of Liz's nagging.

"What I'm going to regret is not getting this speech done before I meet with Dalton."

"My, you're getting chummy. You used to call him the senator. I don't know if it's a good idea to have a crush on your boss."

"It's not a crush. I admire him. He has ambition and integrity."

"Having the one without the other wouldn't be good."

"Having what?"

"'Ambition is a good servant, but a bad master,' William Shakespeare."

"Good quote. I might be able to use that." Maddie jotted it down on an index card.

"As a Christian, it's better to live that," Lizette said.

"Do you think I'm overly ambitious?" Maddie had always considered herself ambitious, but not overly so.

"It can be a fine line. Oh brother! Did you hear what he's doing now?" her sister sounded exasperated.

"Who? Noah?" Poor Noah, Maddie wondered what Lizette's husband could have done to make her so frustrated.

"Noah? No, of course not. President Smith!"

Maddie sighed. She needed to get to work. She should have known it would be hard to get right off the phone. Like many sisters close in age, they were almost complete opposites in looks and temperament. Maddie was blond, took after their mother's Scandinavian side, and had always enjoyed primping and fussing with clothes and her appearance. Lizette had dark red hair, looked Irish like their father, and preferred a simpler style of dress. While Maddie had always loved history, her sister kept up on current events almost religiously.

"What did he do?"

"He's loosening regulations on illegal immigrants... again!" Lizette sounded as though she were taking it personally.

"I'm sorry, Liz, but I've really got to go." Maddie got off as graciously as possible and dropped the phone on the bed. She grabbed her laptop, went back into the living room, and plopped down on the sofa. "Back to work."

The front door to Jay's condo opened; Riley woofed and sprang up, bumping his head on the underside of the table. Barking loudly, he clambered through the dining room chairs, pounding toward the front door, and flattened whoever had come through it. "Who is it?" Jay called out in a singsong voice, knowing very well who it was. The visitor was now lying in the entryway on the tile, being held down by the large dog. It was his best friend, Max, and he was screaming like a teenage girl in a horror movie.

"Help! Get him off me! Get him off! Get him off!" Jay walked around the corner of his sectional couch and sure enough, there was Max pinned to the floor with the former guard dog's fangs near his throat. Jay bent over at the waist laughing, watching Max struggling to push the dog off.

Jay finally said, "Down, Riley." Riley instantly stepped back and sat down.

"How can you have that vicious beast around here? He could have killed me!" Max felt all around his scrawny neck as though checking to see if he were missing part of it.

"Serves you right. You should've knocked." Jay was still smiling as he picked up the papers that had fallen on the floor again and sat down at the table. He started making notes on a yellow legal pad.

"I never knocked before you got him, and you didn't seem to mind." Max smoothed down his always unruly red hair, indignantly pulled out a chair, and sat down, glaring at Riley. "Seems to me a life-long friend shouldn't be attacked when he enters your condo. You've had that dog for months. Why doesn't he know me by now? Don't your neighbors complain about him?"

"My *neighbors* don't come into my condo

without knocking. More than one has told me how much safer they feel, living in a building with a former guard dog nearby. He's extremely well behaved. He barks only when necessary. He's a great dog."

Max looked unconvinced. He held out his hand. It was visibly trembling. "Look at that. I can't stop shaking." He ran his hand over his face.

"That, my friend, is because you are a wimp. You need to start pumping iron, and take up running so you have some wind."

"Whatever, who beat who playing basketball last weekend?"

"Whom."

"Whom?"

"Who beat whom playing..."

"Okay, whatever, name the time, and we'll see who's the king of the court and who's a wimp."

Jay handed the speech to Max. "Read that," he said.

Max started to read the speech, then after a few sentences leafed through it to see how long it was. "What is this?"

"This is the latest speech Senator Stanfield gave." Just thinking about the senator piously mouthing those words in his hypocritical way started Jay pacing across the room, raking his fingers through his thick, dark hair. "He quoted Reagan, just like he agrees with him! The most liberal senator on the Republican side." Jay pointed his finger at Max. "You know he throws every close vote to the Democrats."

Max tossed the pieces of paper on the table. "I

know because you've told me every time Congress convenes how everyone votes, whether I want to hear it or not. By the way, in case you didn't know, it's not. Maybe he doesn't write his speeches."

"I know he doesn't write them. He hired some girl fresh out of college to construct his facade. She's either as corrupt as he is, or she is woefully ignorant of politics, and if she is, D.C. is no place to be. They will eat her alive."

Looking down at her formerly neat piles of cards, Maddie gasped. Wet, coffee-stained paw prints covered her index cards and her coffee table. Her overturned mug was lying in a puddle of coffee that was dripping onto the hardwood floor. She heard the sound of lapping and peered around the table.

"Franky!" Sprawling over the table, she snatched her dachshund from the puddle he was standing in, grabbed a towel, and headed for the bathroom. "You deserve this," she said, putting him into the bathtub and turning on the water. Franky looked panicked and tried to climb out, but she held him down with one hand, and soaped and scrubbed his long fur with the other. "I know you hate this worse than anything, but you should have thought of that before you helped yourself to my coffee." Maddie cupped her hand under Franky's chin, forcing him to look her in the eye. "You have to conquer this addiction before it gets the better of you." Maddie reached for the sprayer and started rinsing him off. "Besides, you've needed a bath for a while, and I love it when you smell like strawberry shampoo." Franky looked pained but stood still while Maddie finished the job, towel-dried him, and set him on the floor. Brushing her thick, dark blond hair out of her eyes, Maddie sighed deeply. "Back to work."

Once free, Franky took off in a blur of red fur. He ran into the kitchen, rubbed himself on the lighthouse rug in front of the sink, ran into the living room, and jumped onto the couch, rubbing his wet fur all over it. "Oh no! Now my house will smell like a wet dog. You get more exercise out of a bath..." Maddie lunged for him, but by then, Franky was standing in the coffee spill, lapping it up again.

Maddie sighed, "Okay, you win. I'll just wipe you off with a wet cloth this time." She painstakingly wiped each paw with a wet washcloth, sponged off her index cards, and mopped up what was left on the table and floor.

Sitting down with her damp cards, Maddie looked at Franky who was now lounging on an afghan in the corner of the couch. "You don't look like you're sorry at all. You made a mess, and you've made me late. Now I'll have to hurry to get this done." Franky turned over on his back and looked at her pathetically. "Why should I rub your belly? You were a bad boy." Maddie picked up her computer and balanced it on her lap ignoring the beseeching look coming from the corner of the couch.

The dachshund rolled over, walked gingerly across the cushion, and started pushing her laptop toward the edge of the couch with his nose. Maddie rescued it just in time. "Oh no! I know that trick. That's how you destroyed my last laptop. Be a good doggy, and let me get my speech written." Franky snuggled next to her, sighed deeply, and closed his eyes.

Maddie logged on, spelling her new password aloud as she typed, "Y-K-N-A-R-F." She looked over at her pup. "Don't get a big head. My password has to be easy to remember, but still be one that no one can figure out."

Maddie pulled up her latest project, a speech the senator was scheduled to give tomorrow. She worked as fast as she could, glancing often at the time. When she was finally done, she adjusted the screen on her laptop, preparing to read it again. "Franky, pay attention. I'm going to try out my speech on you." No matter how good it looked in print, Maddie was never satisfied with a speech until she had voiced it out loud a few times, so she could hear how it sounded.

She launched into the speech, reading it the way she thought the illustrious senator would. She glanced over at Franky. He yawned.

"So you think it's boring, huh? I guess I could liven it up a bit." Maddie changed a few words and read the last paragraph again, with more feeling. She looked at Franky out of the corner of her eye. He jumped off the couch, picked up his chew toy, and after giving her a furtive glance, skulked into the bedroom.

She called after his retreating figure, "Is it that bad? Franky, get back here!"

She stopped and looked around as if someone

might have heard her. She dropped her head into her hands. "What is the matter with me? I'm asking a dog his opinion on a speech! Maybe I have been working too much. I need to get out more." She saved the document and closed her laptop. Just as she was putting it out of reach of tiny dogs, she heard the muffled ring of her cell phone and ran to the bedroom to frantically search for her phone in the rumpled sheets.

Fumbling to answer, she almost hung up on her boss. "Hello, this is Maddie." She waited expectantly for his deep, authoritative voice.

"Hello Madison, this is Dalton," the now-familiar and welcome voice always seemed out of place booming from her small phone. For some reason, he spoke louder than necessary on cell phones as though his voice had to carry across the miles through sheer volume because there were no wires attached. "I'm going to need that speech earlier than I thought. Can you meet me at The Daily Grind in an hour?"

Her relief that she had the speech finished was instantly replaced by anxiety at the thought of seeing her boss at a place other than his office. They usually conducted all of their conferences there. Seeing him in such an informal setting was unusual. She assured him she could be there within the hour and hurriedly got off the phone so she could get ready.

A change of venue called for a change of wardrobe. What should she wear? She ran to her closet, grabbed some clothes off the rod, and threw them on the bed, still on the hangers. She started holding outfits up in front of herself turning a critical eye to the mirror. "I want him to see me as a professional, so maybe I should wear the type of clothes I usually wear. But it would be nice if he could see me in casual clothes; then maybe he could relax around me and see me as more than just an employee." Maddie held up garment after garment. Her favorite midnight blue suit was a contender. She compared it to the jeans and T-shirt lying on the bed. "I guess I'd better stick with looking like a professional." She grabbed a white blouse out of the pile.

Franky had darted under the chair while she was choosing an outfit. "Don't worry, Buddy. I'm done speechwriting for now, besides I wouldn't think of interrupting your important chewing. But in the future," she tossed over her shoulder just before she closed the bathroom door, "you might want to remember my paycheck from this job makes all of this possible." She gave a dramatic, sweeping gesture and turned on the shower.

Dalton hung up the phone and smiled. He always liked to go to the next level in a relationship, to see how far it would go. Madison had been writing his speeches for a few months, and they'd always met in his office. Last week, he'd asked Jeanie if she knew Madison's favorite coffee shop. Jeanie said that Madison mentioned liking the Daily Grind, so he'd picked that spot to meet today. He wanted a more intimate setting to loosen her up. She was so business-like here. He could tell she liked him from her nervousness, even though she maintained a professional attitude. He was planning on arranging more of their meetings outside the office.

He looked at himself in the full-length mirror attached to the inside of his coat closet door, straightened his tie, and rubbed his hand over his closely-shaven face. Even though approaching 40, he knew he'd easily pass for being in his early 30s if it wasn't for the fact that he wouldn't have met the age requirements for being a senator when he finished the late Senator Sinclair's term.

There was about an hour before he'd arranged to meet her. This would be a good time to catch up on his emails. He brought up his account on his laptop, read and answered a few emails before noticing the one from his liaison with the Democratic National Committee. He couldn't meet with anyone from the DNC directly, and it was iffy just receiving emails from this person, but all the email told him was the code name for a spot where a note would be dropped. All of this undercover spy stuff seemed like this was a silly 60s secret agent movie. Nobody cared about party politics anymore. Checking his watch, he saw he wouldn't have time to pick up the message before he met Madison. He stood up, about to leave for the Daily Grind when Jeanie called him on his intercom.

"Yes, Jeanie?" the senator struggled to keep his impatience in check. Jeanie was barely competent. She still hadn't given him that file. He would've fired her a long time ago and replaced her with someone younger, prettier, and better at the job, but he owed a relative of hers a favor.

"There is a young lady here to see you, sir."

"Who is it, Jeanie?" Wasn't it obvious he would need to know who it was to know if he wanted to meet with her? Why did she have to be told such basic things?

"Her name is Tiffany Roberts. She's the aide to…"

"Never mind, Jeanie. I know whose aide she is. Send her in." Dalton smiled and almost rubbed his hands with glee. Tiffany was a knockout. He just might have to make a little change in plans. He could meet Madison later and take Tiffany to an early lunch now. And since it was business, he wouldn't have to spend a dime of his own. The government would foot the bill.

The man must have hired a decorator, Tiffany thought as Jeanie showed her into Senator Stanfield's lavish office. Tiffany eyed the groupings of tasteful art. Richly upholstered leather furniture was featured throughout including the elegant chair behind the massive desk. The man liked the finer things in life. She'd chosen the right recipient for her information. He could afford it.

The senator rose and walked toward her with a gleam in his eye. Men often had that look when they saw her, Tiffany knew. She counted on it. With catlike precision, she walked noiselessly toward him extending her hand. With every move, her choreographed steps were more like those of a dancer than a low-level senator's staff worker. She dressed to entice and often saw men's eyes drawn exactly to where she guided them. She never hesitated to look any man squarely in the eye, no matter what lie was rolling off her tongue, but she usually didn't have to.

Dalton held onto her hand a few seconds longer than was customary for a handshake, and that was all she needed to know. The right presentation and he would be hooked. She smiled. It didn't reach her eyes, but it never did.

After Jeanie had closed the door, Tiffany said, "I'm a little surprised you'd have an assistant like that. Paying back a favor?"

"Maybe. Why? Do you want the job?"

"I've set my sights higher." Tiffany walked over to the overstuffed couch, stroked the leather, and continued to run her hand over the smooth mahogany table.

"How high?" Dalton asked, following her around the room with his eyes.

"High. Take me to lunch, and I'll tell you what I have in mind."

"I was just about to leave to meet my speechwriter," he said.

"Madison McPherson? You're not meeting her here? Trying to bump things up a notch?"

"I don't know what you mean."

He didn't fool Tiffany. "Trust me, it won't work. She's a prude."

"Unlike you..."

"Unlike me. Well, you have plans..." Tiffany started to leave.

Dalton stopped her with his hand on the door. "Nothing I can't postpone. Lunch with you seems more, shall we say, promising."

"I promise you, you'll be very glad you took this lunch."

As if Jay's remark about D.C. eating the speechwriter reminded Max of his empty stomach, he moved into the kitchen and opened the refrigerator door. "You got anything to eat?"

Jay sat down, picked up his pen, and started taking notes again. "Sure, help yourself. You know where everything is."

Max came back with an open takeout container, poking at the contents with a fork. "What is this, Mongolian beef?"

"Man, it's Szechwan chicken." Jay threw down his pen and looked at his friend in disbelief. "Can't you tell the difference between chicken and beef?"

"Not when it's covered with a gooey brown sauce. Did you eat out of this?" Max sniffed cautiously.

"Of course I ate out of it; it was my dinner last night." Jay wrote something on the yellow legal pad, scratched it out, and rewrote it. "You know you don't care about germs. Go ahead and eat it."

Max carried the Asian food over to the black sectional and looked around. "I never noticed it before, but this place is kind of scary."

"That's because you almost had your throat ripped out by a German shepherd."

"No, I mean it. Everything in here is black or silver or glass. It's kind of cold and impersonal."

"What do you want, flowers and lace? I'm a guy!"

Riley walked over to peer in the food container. Max turned his back on the dog and kept eating.

"Give him a bite, and he'll be your friend for life," Jay suggested.

"Nah. I've fed him before, and it hasn't helped." Max finished the food and tossed the Styrofoam container on the coffee table.

"Hey, throw that away. This isn't your apartment, you know."

Max picked up the to-go box and headed toward the garbage can in the kitchen. "Yeah, I know. This is your 'living space' and you like to keep it 'livable.'"

"Did you come over just to bum food off me?" Jay opened his laptop and started typing from the notes on his legal pad.

Max brightened. "No. I also came over to see if I could bum money off you. Got a twenty you're not using?"

Jay pulled out his wallet, peered inside, and fingered the bills. He and Max had grown up together. Jay had no siblings, and Max had always been like a brother to him. They'd frequently relied on each other as they got into and out of scrapes together as kids. Max had even lent him part of the down payment on Jay's first car, a beat-up 1968 Cougar that Jay wished he still had and could restore now that he had an income. "I could lend you fifteen. I'm about to run out for coffee, and I haven't had supper yet."

"Yeah, and trust me, you don't have anything left to eat in your refrigerator." Max accepted the bills and shoved them in his shorts pocket. "It's weird that you still use money, Jay. Ever heard of debit cards?"

"If someone gets your debit card, they can clean out your bank account, and it's such a hassle to get it back."

"Well, you are a dinosaur, carrying cash."

"If I wasn't, you wouldn't be borrowing money from me. I wouldn't give you a debit or credit card."

"You should restock your refrigerator, too. Don't you ever go to the grocery store?"

Jay smiled, "What would I do with groceries? Do I look like a chef?"

"We should shoot hoops later. You'll need to work off all that anger you have for Senator Stanford."

"Sure, and it's Stanfield."

"I can't keep them straight. There's like a hundred of them."

"There's exactly one hundred, Max. How could you live in D.C. and not know that? Haven't you ever had a civics course?"

Jay opened the coat closet to get his jacket. Max peered around him at the inside of the closet. "It is unreal how neat you are. You're supposed to throw all of your junk in here. That's why these closets are near the front door. And yeah, I had a civics course a million years ago. And like most people, I forgot everything I learned. Nobody knows this stuff unless they're politicians, teachers, or journalists like you."

Jay shook his head. "People who care what

direction this country is going know 'this stuff.' What would happen if most of the people just forgot?"

"You know, I'd think if you were going to single out a corrupt politician to investigate, the obvious choice would be the president. People are calling him a dictator. And the way the price of gas has gone up has everyone mad at him."

Jay shrugged. "He's on his way out. He's ticked off too many people. Even the Democrats won't support him. Last year he refused to support an act that was voted in by Congress and signed into law by the last president. And don't get me started on his exorbitant use of Executive Orders. You know those are supposed to be used to direct federal agencies to support laws already voted in by Congress, not to make his own laws."

This subject was obviously the last thing Max wanted to discuss since he hurried over to the door and yanked it open. "Well, I'd love to stay here all night talking politics with you, but I've got to run."

"Wait up, I'll walk down with you," Jay said and followed him down the stairs.

But Max said "See you!" took the stairs two at a time and was pulling out of the parking lot before Jay had his car door unlocked. It didn't occur to him until he reached the coffee shop, that Max had never said why he needed the money.

The meeting with Tiffany was going exceptionally well. She'd suggested they continue their little tête-à-tête off the premises, mirroring his thoughts. She might be only an aide, but she had followed the axiom "dress for the job you want, not the job you have" to the utmost degree. That was one thing about Madison McPherson he'd never understood. Dalton had always felt, if you've got it, flaunt it, but Madison dressed like his grandmother. She looked good, she had taste, but she was so modest. What a waste!

Tiffany, on the other hand, understood the way a woman should look. Packaging was everything, and a little flirting in private never hurt her chances either. He looked at her again, pleased at what he saw. Maybe she'd heard he was on the lookout for another staff member. He wasn't, but he didn't have to let that cat out of the bag right away. He could put her to good use. In the meantime, he needed to cancel his meeting with Madison.

Three

The sky was overcast as Maddie approached the Daily Grind. Her phone rang. She paused by the side of the shop and tucked her long, dark blond hair behind her ear as she answered.

"Hi Liz, I can't talk long. I'm just arriving at the coffee shop."

"Oh yeah, you're meeting your boss. Well, remember I've advised you do some investigating to make sure he's going in the right direction."

Maddie started to move toward the door just as a man came around the end of the block heading toward her.

"Speaking of the right direction, there is a super cute guy coming my way."

"Maybe you should have coffee with Super Cute Guy instead," Lizette said teasingly.

"Maybe. I think I've seen Super Cute Guy in here before. Gotta go!" Maddie whispered and hung up the phone. She watched as the dark-haired man approached. She had seen him in The Daily Grind before. Suddenly a red cardinal flew by her and smashed into the window of the coffee shop.

"Oh!" Maddie jumped back. The dazed bird lay there for a moment; then it picked itself up and stood there as though trying to regain its sense of balance. Maddie was unsure if the bird needed help. The Cute Guy must have had the same thought. He started after the bird who took flight before he could reach it.

Well, that settled that, Maddie thought. The

bird was out of sight immediately. Maddie could already smell the delicious scent of freshly ground coffee. She always enjoyed the first, almost overwhelmingly luscious whiff of coffee that flowed out the door, but it was beginning to rain so she hurried to enter. Cute Guy held the door for her. There was already a long line forming, and she quickly took her place in it. Cute Guy had a muscular build and had smiled while he held the door for her; then got behind her in line. She'd always wondered at the etiquette of such situations. He would've been ahead of her if he weren't such a gentleman. She got another peek at him by pretending to look out the window as if she were meeting someone, which she was. Yep, the man behind her was pretty good-looking, dressed in jeans and a corduroy sport coat. Suddenly, she just blurted it out. "Would you like to get in front of me?"

He seemed very surprised by her offer. Now she felt she had to explain herself, but Maddie had the unfortunate tendency to get nervous around handsome guys, then say everything as fast as she could, going off on crazy tangents, so it all came out in a rush, and later she wasn't sure if the words were even in the right order. "See I've often thought how unfair it is for the polite person who holds the door for someone to lose his or her place in line. You got the door for me, so I got through it first, and I got in line before you did even though you got here first." By the look on his face, it was obvious he thought she was crazy. She quickly edited her words. How many times did she say "got" anyway? Should she try to explain it again, only speak slower? With his dark hair and eyes, he could be a foreigner. He probably didn't even speak English!

The guy spoke slowly as though he could control her rate of speech with his own, "No. I'm fine."

"Oh, good." Maddie turned around wishing she'd arrived a few minutes later and missed this conversation entirely. What must he think of her? Now she felt an explanation was in order, why she talked so fast and said such gobbledygook. Well, no way was she telling him that he made her nervous because of his looks. I'm sure he knows how attractive he is anyway. Wait, did she say that out loud, for the entire world and Cute Guy to hear? Maddie glanced around. No one was looking at her as if she were a lunatic. She must have only thought it was spoken. Was she losing it? It must be all those conversations with her dog. Well, one-sided conversations, "He doesn't actually talk back."

Who doesn't talk back?"

Maddie turned around. Cute Guy was looking at her expectantly. He said it again, "Who doesn't talk back?"

"Um, that would be my dog, Franky," she admitted.

Cute Guy nodded. "No. I guess he wouldn't."

Maddie nodded, too. "No, he wouldn't." She turned back around. Well, that should firmly cement her in his mind as an idiot. She determined not to say another word or think another thought except coffee until it was her turn to order. Medium latte. Medium latte. Medium latte. Medium latte.

Maddie moved up in line, medium latte, medium latte, medium...

"What can I get you?" The barista's fingers were poised over the register.

"I'd like a medium cute guy, please, extra hot." Maddie immediately clamped her hand over her mouth.

"I'd like one, too, especially if he's extra hot," the girl behind the counter smiled, "but I meant your drink order."

"I'd like a me-medium latte," she stammered, then practically whispered, "extra hot."

"For here or to go?"

Maddie longed to say "to go" so she could escape. "For here," Maddie said reluctantly. She paid for the drink and hurried off. It was such a relief to get away from the line after embarrassing herself. The farther away from that guy she could get, the better.

Carrying her chunky, white porcelain mug filled to the brim with the latte nicely foamed, Maddie looked around for just the right table for her meeting with Dalton. It needed to be secluded enough so they could discuss his next speech intimately and without interruption, but not obviously so. She found a spot and unpacked her laptop. She logged on, mouthing her new password. Then she cautiously took a sip of her latte but decided it was still a little too hot to drink.

Maddie leaned back and looked around at the Daily Grind with pleasure. She loved this place. It must be Dalton's favorite, too, for him to suggest they meet here. She'd found the coffee shop in her neighborhood right after arriving in Washington. Housed in one of the older buildings, it was very small but had high ceilings, making it seem bigger than it was. The decorating was reminiscent of a turn of the century newspaper, with an old-fashioned printing press hung on the wall in the back. It had dark green walls and restored wood throughout. Maddie loved it. Quaint with great coffee, it was a wonderful combination.

She heard Cute Guy talking on his cell behind her. He'd stopped at the condiment stand. She took a glance over her shoulder hoping he'd sit somewhere else or better yet, take his coffee to go when he finished his call.

Her phone rang while she was contemplating moving to another table. Pulling out her cell, she saw it was her boss again.

"Madison, this is Dalton." Maddie held the phone away from her ear to keep from being deafened by his booming voice. "Something's come up, and I'll have to meet with you another time. It'll have to be tomorrow. Can you meet me at the office early?"

Maddie was disappointed but tried not to sound that way. "Of course, Senator, no problem."

"Since I have you on the phone, could you give me a short outline of what's in the latest speech?"

Maddie brought up the document on her computer. "Well, you'd wanted to mention the last bill you voted for to lower taxes."

Dalton said quickly, "Did you mention it was

defeated by the Democratic majority?"

"Yes, sir, I put in the exact count the Democrats defeated it by. Also, I put in your speech those specific social programs you're hoping to add to a future piece of legislation," and she read off the list of his pet projects.

There was a pause before Dalton's voice came over the phone somewhat tersely, "Uh, Madison, where did you get that list? I didn't give that to you."

Maddie was surprised by the annoyed tone in his voice. She hoped she hadn't done anything wrong. "I'm sorry. It was on the desk next to the notes you gave me for this speech. I thought it was meant to be included, too."

Equally surprising was how quickly Dalton's voice changed back. It came smoothly over the phone. "Let's leave that out for right now. Can you put in some more conservative quotes? You know, use the founding fathers' sayings to show how much I support freedom and courage, how much I love America. Did you get the specifics from the contact at the university on the length allowed on the speech?"

Maddie pulled a piece of paper out of her satchel, "Yes. It's not a lot of time, but I know you like to keep your speeches pretty short anyway."

"Yes, I want to leave time for the audience to meet me. Well, that should be a good start. If you can arrive about half an hour early, that should do it."

Maddie nodded. "Yes, that should do it."

Dalton got off the phone, and Maddie put hers

slowly back in her purse considering the speech that now needed rewriting. Suddenly Maddie's day seemed empty. She was looking forward to getting to know her boss outside of the office for the first time. The informal setting might have helped to bring them a little closer to a non-working relationship. He sometimes came off as a little overbearing, but that could be just a façade, a bravado he put on for the public eye. She wanted to get to know the real Dalton Stanfield.

Time for a to-go cup. No use staying around here any longer. It was too noisy to get much work done. She picked up her coffee mug, taking a step and turning around in one motion. She didn't see Cute Guy, who was right behind her at the condiment stand until she ran into him, splashing her entire hot latte down the whole right sleeve of his jacket!

The man quickly took a step back, bent over, and shook his arm, trying to rid himself of the hot liquid. Maddie gasped in horror at what she'd done, grabbed napkins out of the dispenser, and started frantically wiping his sleeve.

"Oh, I am so sorry! I can't believe I spilled that all over you! Oh, and it was extra hot! Did I burn you?"

Spilled-on-Guy reached around her and grabbed his phone and other things off the condiment stand, pocketing them quickly, while Maddie continued to sponge off his arm. "No no, it's okay. I'm not burned. It's not your fault. You didn't see me."

Maddie grabbed her purse, "Please let me pay

to get your jacket dry cleaned. Do you think the stain will come out? I'll pay for a new jacket if it won't come out. I am so sorry!"

Spilled-on-Guy held up his hands and started backing away. "No. You don't owe me a thing. I'm fine." He turned and bolted from the shop, got in a car, and drove quickly away. A barista hurried over with a towel and started wiping up her mess.

Maddie's rush of adrenaline had left with Spilled-on-Guy. She felt deflated. What a klutz! And what was with all the spilled coffee today? Maddie started packing her things in her satchel, before remembering she could have been splattered with coffee too. After examining her clothes, she was amazed there wasn't a stain on her favorite blue suit. What a relief! She'd bought it with her first check as a speechwriter, and it was not cheap.

There was no need for a to-go cup now. "I think I've had enough coffee for today, anyway," she said aloud without thinking.

"That's for sure," a guy at a neighboring table said pointedly.

She grabbed her things indignantly, absentmindedly picking up a scrap of yellow paper that was on the floor, stuffed it in her satchel, and hurried to the door. She knew she would never return to The Daily Grind and left without taking a last look around.

Dalton walked over to his desk to check the piles of paper. The list Madison had mentioned was gone. Dalton wanted to explode, but he had to maintain a calm exterior with Tiffany in the room.

He hadn't meant to leave that paper where anyone would see it! Why would Madison think he'd want to mention those programs in a speech? It was a good thing she was so naive. Anyone else in Washington would have known right away that only liberals would be involved in supporting those programs. He knew many of his cronies didn't care as much as they publicly claimed to about helping the poor or uneducated. Money invested in pet programs meant more power and more favors returned. Keeping them dependent on government programs was how to keep their votes. It was all part of the political game, and he knew how to play it better than anyone did. He was tired of his limited resources and influence as a senator. "It's the only game in town, and I'm going to keep on playing it until I've reached the highest office," he said to himself. "Always take it to the next level."

Dalton smiled and held the door open for Tiffany to walk through. He forced himself to concentrate on the woman before him. After all, there was no use dwelling on unpleasant things with such enticing possibilities stretching out ahead of him for the rest of the day.

Four

Jay gunned the motor to get as far away from The Daily Grind as fast as he could. Soon, though, he slowed down a bit since the streets were still wet. He awkwardly shrugged out of his wet jacket while steering with his leg. Fortunately, he had on a short-sleeved shirt that didn't have too much coffee spilled on it, and most of it had been near the cuff on the jacket. He'd have to drop off his coat at the dry cleaner later. He was in too much of a hurry right now.

He couldn't believe his luck. He'd just been talking to Max about Senator Stanfield's new speechwriter when barely ten minutes later he'd run into her, literally, or rather she'd run into him.

He'd seen the attractive young woman many times before at that same coffee shop, not knowing who she was, of course. He'd thought she was pretty, noticing she was usually wearing a dress and always looked classic. He'd almost introduced himself to her the last time he saw her. Now he was glad he hadn't and not only because she was the senator's speechwriter.

"What a ditz!" he said aloud. He'd tried to follow the whole "I go first, you go first," spiel, and immediately wondered how English could be her first language. It wasn't her fault, though, that she'd spilled coffee all over him, since he'd been huddled close behind her, eavesdropping on her conversation and taking notes. He stopped to consider the ethics of his actions as he was inserting his key into the lock of his condo. Jay decided he was justified in what he'd done. It was a public place, and she didn't seem to be trying to hold her conversation down. He could hear Dalton Stanfield's voice, too. He spoke so loudly, Jay could even make out her name, "Madison."

Riley met him at the door, but Jay barely acknowledged his presence. He went directly to his dining room table and sat down to reread the speech, although he'd read it so many times, he could almost give it from memory now. He couldn't ignore the dichotomy. How could that woman write this speech? She could barely put two sentences together without tripping over her words. "Let alone the people around her," he said, and then felt guilty all over again for letting her take the blame for the spill.

But he could hardly believe what had fallen into his lap while he stopped for a simple brewed coffee. How fortunate to be privy to that list of programs the senator was planning on sponsoring. It was obvious she didn't know what it meant for a Republican senator to support such liberal programs. She probably wasn't corrupt; she was just ignorant.

Jay looked around now for his coffee. He must have left it at The Daily Grind. He'd also forgotten to get something to eat. Well, that would have to wait. He had something to do first. He quickly changed his shirt. Then he pulled out the notes he'd scribbled at the coffee shop, grabbed his yellow legal pad, and started writing. He needed to change the direction of his column.

Dalton and Tiffany entered Circa, an elite restaurant in Dupont Circle. He held her chair for her as she was seated, and took one across from her at the small bistro table. Even though the table was very small, she still scooted a little closer, "so we can talk privately" she said and pressed her knee against his. Dalton was ready to promise her the job right there.

He figured Tiffany couldn't be more than 25, so if she were going to flirt with him, someone nearly 15 years her senior, he was sure she wanted something. What was she up to?

Tiffany rearranged the silverware neatly on her cloth napkin. She brushed her straight, shiny black hair out of her perfectly made-up eyes, looked around the busy restaurant, and leaned in closely to whisper. Again, Dalton felt as though he were in a spy movie. He couldn't help but notice her plunging neckline, not that he tried avoiding it. She whispered, "I have an offer that I think will benefit both of us."

He was intrigued. This could be anything. He leaned toward her, their heads almost touching. "Go on."

Tiffany said, "I've come across a communiqué recently in which I think you will be greatly interested. I have supporting documents for this, too." She opened her purse and removed a piece of paper. She unfolded it and slid it across the table.

Dalton was a little disappointed that Tiffany was being so business-like. He had been hoping this meeting would benefit him in other ways. He picked up the piece of paper, started reading, and looked sharply at Tiffany. "Where did you get this?" he asked.

Tiffany looked him steadily in the eye. "I have my sources," she said.

"Are your 'sources' reliable?" He studied her, trying to gauge if she could be trusted.

Tiffany never blinked. "Absolutely," she said.

Dalton was no novice at politics. "Why did you choose me to share this with?"

Tiffany took a slow drink from her glass of water. "I've heard you have certain, shall we say, leanings, which make you an excellent recipient for this information."

Dalton nodded. Tiffany might be connected with the DNC, too. He couldn't believe his luck; this information was the break he had been waiting for. He turned the paper over to see if there was anything written on the other side. Then he reread the short paragraph. He looked at Tiffany over the top of the paper. What would she want for something this valuable? What was he willing to give for it?

Maddie trudged up the steps under the dripping eaves, and let herself into her apartment. She wasn't sure if her weariness was due to her severe lack of caffeine or to the roller coaster ride of a day she'd had. "And it's barely noon!" She said in dismay. She dropped her satchel and purse on the couch and picked up Franky who had met her at the door wagging his tail. All of the trouble he'd caused her that morning was forgiven for the comfort she felt as she hugged him.

Maddie put the small dog down and hung up her favorite blue suit. She changed into sweats and a T-shirt.

Needing more comforting, Maddie made herself a cup of hot chocolate and turned on the TV as a distraction from the thoughts she couldn't stop from coming. TCM was her favorite station and was one of the few luxuries she allowed herself until her school loans were paid. Turning to the station now, she thought how simple life seemed in old movies, how perfect. Everything was so clean. Women wore beautiful gowns; all the men wore suits, and every problem worked out in the end. Snuggled with Franky, she fell asleep on the couch.

A knock came at the door while Jay was furiously scribbling. "Come in," he called, continuing to write without looking up.

Max cautiously put his head through the door. "It's me, Max."

Jay looked up. "Yeah, I know. I said, 'Come in.'"

"I was talking to the dog," Max said, the rest of his gangly form now visible as he stepped through the door, closed it slowly, and gingerly crept to the table. He pulled out a chair and sat next to Jay.

He looked at Max pointedly. "You know Riley can see you, right? You don't have to tiptoe around him."

Max spoke quietly, "Yeah, I know. I just don't want to upset him. You want to shoot some hoops, now?"

"I can't. Man, I just got a scoop on a great story. Let me tell you what happened," and he gave Max all the details.

"You know what you should have said when Madison offered to pay for your jacket?" Max said when Jay finished relating the incident.

"What?"

"You should have told her you had a number in mind, and you were accepting only that number. Then when she asked what it was, you should have said, 'your phone number.'" Max grinned.

Jay looked at him in disbelief. "Did you hear any of what I said? She's a menace to society and frankly, she has to be stupid. Why would I want her digits?"

"Man, that's harsh. Maybe she's not as stupid as you think. Okay, she's not a political genius like you. I'm not into politics, either. Do you think I'm stupid?"

"No Max, but your job is to work with computers. Her job is to understand the way politics work in D.C."

"No. Her job is to write pretty speeches for the senator to say. So while she may be too trusting and not a good judge of character, that doesn't make her stupid. Also, if she wasn't so innocent, she wouldn't have read off the good senator's liberal agenda in a D.C. coffee shop for all the world and you to hear so you could write your story and let the rest of us in on it. Whether we want to be or not," Max added under his breath.

Jay considered what Max said, "Okay. We'll call her naïve, but I'm still not asking her out. I've already googled he, and found out her last name. It's McPherson. I could probably get her number from the senator's assistant at the Capitol, if I wanted it, which I don't."

"Dude, you are way too picky. No wonder you're in your 30s and still not married," Max shook his head and got up to leave.

"You know I'm not in my 30s. We're the same age. Incidentally, I don't see you dating a whole lot either," Jay pointed out while he kept writing.

"You know I'm shy around women. Besides, dating is like going fishing. I don't want to have to keep throwing back the ones that aren't keepers. I'm waiting for just the right one to come along before I throw in my line and start reeling her in," Max grinned and pantomimed fly-fishing.

Jay laughed, "Throw in your line? I don't know any women who would find that analogy particularly flattering."

"Hey, I didn't mean women are a bunch of smelly fish. It's like, remember back at Camp Lanateesee, how they were always saying, 'Don't date anyone you wouldn't want for a mate,'? Like that."

"Camp Lanateesee? I haven't thought of that place in years. I'm surprised you would even bring it up."

Max looked uncomfortable. "Yeah, well, I only brought it up as an example about dating."

"Remember the Legend of Lake Lanateesee?"

"Uh, no, not really. Maybe I should be going, Jay." Max moved toward the door.

Jay lowered his voice down to a spooky

whisper. "Remember we would all sit around the campfire and the camp counselors would tell us the Legend of Lake Lanateesee. And we knew some night when we were asleep in our bunks, the Skeleton of the Lake was going to creep out from its watery grave and place its icy cold finger on your lips, to silence you forever." Jay reached out slowly with one finger toward Max's lips.

"Cut it out, Jay! You never believed that dumb legend and neither did I!"

Jay laughed and drew his hand back.

"They sure told good ghost stories at Camp Lanateesee. And they gave good dating advice too, didn't they? Sure, I might be a little too particular," Jay admitted. "I never claimed to be perfect, but at least I'm lucid. The woman talked gibberish." He stopped typing and looked through his papers. "Uh oh."

"What?" Max stopped with his hand on the doorknob and wiped his forehead.

"A piece must have torn off one page of the notes I took. I can't find the missing piece." Jay looked through every pocket in his pants and jacket.

"Is it important?"

"Well, I think I can make out what I meant without it, but I wish I had it."

Max pulled open the door. "Well, no matter what anyone says, I won't call you 'stupid' for losing it." Max waved and closed the door behind him.

Five

Dalton watched Tiffany take a bite of her salmon salad, and marveled that someone so young could be so cold and calculating. She hadn't backed down a bit when he'd grilled her trying to discover how she'd come across such sensitive information. He had to know it was real and that he could trust her. Watching her cut her salad into tiny bites with the precision of a surgeon gave him a chill. He watched her take another bite.

He couldn't even eat the petite filet mignon sliders he'd ordered. He was too excited. Finally a chance to advance his career! Sure, someone else would have to bow out, but everyone knew the president was on his way down the pike already. He was growing increasingly unpopular, as he'd pushed through project after project without congressional approval as if he thought he was king.

Imagine... the presidency! Well, he would probably have to settle for the vice-presidency right now, but that could be a stepping-stone to the highest office. If only he could trust Tiffany.

Maddie woke up, feeling like a slug, with Franky licking her face, a sure sign he wanted to go out. Since it had stopped raining, she put his leash on him, grabbed her key, and stepped outside. The trees were still dripping a few drops here and there, but Frank didn't seem to mind. Maybe she should walk him around the block a time or two to clear her head after that nap. With all the hours she'd been putting in at her job, she hadn't had much exercise lately, and she'd noticed her clothes were getting a little snug. In the past, they'd frequently gone to a park near her apartment. Right now, a brief walk was all she could muster.

Jay closed his laptop. He'd finished writing that piece in record time and had submitted it to his editor, but it was getting late, and he still hadn't had anything to eat. Since the rain had ended, he decided to go for a quick run with Riley before supper. He knew he wouldn't want to exercise for a while after he ate. He changed, snapped on Riley's leash, and headed for their favorite park.

Unlike many runners, Jay didn't listen to music while he ran. He used the time to sort out things in his head. He thought back to the conversation he'd overheard. Remembering the disappointment in Madison's voice, he was convinced that it was not of an employee wanting to share her work with her boss. It sounded more like a woman in love with a man who was standing her up. Maybe that explained why she was so easy to manipulate. "Love is blind," Jay muttered under his breath. She seemed like a nice enough girl. It was too bad she hadn't chosen a better man to fall for.

Maddie and Franky had circled the block once and were almost done with the second and final lap, when a jogger rounded the corner, running toward them with a large German shepherd on a leash. It was him! Cute, Spilled-on-Guy! What would he think, running into her again like this? Maddie knew exactly what he'd think. That she'd set this up, that she was following him. He already thought she had a screw loose. That was evident by the way he ran out of the coffee shop at breakneck speed. Maddie did the only thing she had time to do. She grabbed Franky and jumped behind the bushes. Franky let out a yelp, so Maddie clamped her hand around his snout.

Out of the corner of his eye, Jay had seen someone fall behind the bushes and heard a yelp of pain. It looked like she'd twisted her ankle. Maybe she needed help. Slowing to a walk, he shortened Riley's leash and walked around the bush. Jay could only stare. The last person he expected to see crouched in the wet grass, muzzling a dog in her arms, her face stuffed in a bush was Madison, the Crazy Coffee Lady.

Maddie could feel him looking at her before she heard him clear his throat. There was no use in explaining. She'd tried that at the coffee shop, and look how great that had turned out. She would have stood up, and exited gracefully, but her long hair was caught in the branches of the bush, and she'd tried, but couldn't untangle herself with Franky in her arms. The little dog had caught sight of the giant German shepherd and had frantically clawed his way up, scratching her neck, until he was huddled up under her chin like a treed cat. The Cute Guy silently helped her get her hair untangled.

She whispered "thank you" and stumbled off with her dog in her arms, the leash trailing uselessly behind her.

Jay watched Madison walk away. He'd never seen someone who needed so much rescuing "from herself," he said softly. How could she get herself into such situations? He'd read her speeches. They were well planned, intelligent. Yet here she was crawling around in the bushes right after it rained. If she wanted to "run into him," again she could have planned it better. It was obvious that she was following him, but he was sure she didn't suspect he was a reporter.

Riley sniffed the bush Madison had been tangled in and pawed at it. Something shiny glinted in the thick leaves. Hanging from a branch was a green, coiled wristband with a key dangling from it. Jay pulled it off and put it around his wrist. He was about to jog after her, but she was nowhere in sight. The sky was starting to look like it held more rain.

Jay shrugged and headed for home. After all, the way this day was going, he was likely to run into her again. If not, he could drop the key off at the senator's office.

"Restraining order," Maddie said firmly and put Franky on the ground when they were far enough away from the scary German shepherd that the tiny dachshund had stopped trembling. "I'm sure he's on the verge of slapping a restraining order on me if we run into each other one more time." A terrible thought occurred to her; he must live in this neighborhood. She was likely to run into him repeatedly! Maddie had chosen this particular neighborhood because she could walk to restaurants, parks, and coffeehouses. Was she going to be forced into hiding in her apartment because she had spilled coffee on someone? Maddie straightened her shoulders. "I live in this neighborhood, too," she said, "and I will not sneak around like I've done something wrong."

She marched up the stairs and was about to unlock her door when she realized her key wasn't around her wrist anymore. She nodded. "Par for the course today." Living alone in a strange city with no family around had worried her so she was prepared in case she was ever locked out of her apartment. She headed for the spot in the landscaping done in rocks where she'd tucked an extra house key in a hide-a-key rock. She also had a car key in a magnetic box under the frame of her car in case she locked her keys in her car.

But which rock was it? It looked like someone had raked them to even them out since she'd placed it there when she moved in a few months ago. She got down on her hands and knees and crawled around looking for the right one. Hearing a clap of thunder, she looked up. "And I would not lay any bets against getting struck by lightning today," she said grimly. Looking toward a particularly large stone at the end, which she was sure was it, she crawled quickly toward it. "Found it!" She called out gleefully. Just as she was stretching toward it, she noticed that a pair of feet had joined her.

Jay saw he wouldn't beat the rain unless he hurried, but as he passed a stone cottage covered with ivy down the street from his condo complex, he noticed a bedraggled figure in the backyard who looked all too familiar, crawling around by the rocks. Almost afraid to approach her, but feeling he had to since he knew she was locked out, Jay jogged over as it started to rain. He stopped next to her as she reached for a large rock with a cry of joy.

Since she was unable to pretend she hadn't seen him, Maddie picked up Franky, who was cowering and whimpering behind her, and turned to face him. What was he doing here anyway? Just who was stalking whom?

Cute Guy held out her house key. "Is this yours?" he asked. "I found it in the bush you got your hair tangled in."

"Thank you," Maddie accepted the key from him. She felt the need to explain but was afraid to open her mouth, so they just stood there in the rain. He didn't look at her as if she were crazy this time, and he didn't look away. She felt like he was seeing her, the real her, for the first time, but she wasn't sure why she felt that way. And she couldn't imagine why he should.

Standing in the drizzling rain, he looked good, very good, just a little wet. Life was so unfair. She knew how she looked without a mirror - grungy from crawling around in the dirty grass, soaking wet, snarled hair. Her makeup was probably all but washed away except for her mascara, which ought to be finding its way down her cheeks right about now. She must look like a longhaired, wet raccoon.

"I'd hidden a spare key out here. I was looking for it." She gestured toward the rocks with her head, a little surprised she hadn't started talking too fast and making a fool of herself as she usually did around good-looking guys. Maybe she could talk to him normally now because she'd embarrassed herself just about as much as any one person could.

Jay turned to go, "Well, I'd better let you two get in the house. You're getting soaked."

Maddie nodded and headed up her stairs. Wet and cold, all she wanted was to soak away this day in a long, hot bath. She still had to rewrite the speech before her meeting tomorrow with Dalton, but maybe that wouldn't take very long. Maddie turned around and watched the Guy with the Penetrating Stare jog away. Would she ever see him again? Why did she want to after all that had happened today? She let herself into her apartment, closed the heavy door, and leaned her forehead against it. Would she ever know his real name, or would she have to keep inventing them?

Six

Dalton stood at his office window watching the rain make its way down the glass. When he'd returned, he'd told Jeanie to hold his calls. He had to make a decision and make it quickly. Tiffany wanted an answer tonight.

It was a simple choice. Use the information or refuse Tiffany's offer. If he used it, he was going to have to give Tiffany a substantial amount of money. At the restaurant, he'd already offered her a position in the new administration as payment, but she must not have much faith in his ability to make that happen. She didn't even bother with the old "a bird in the hand is worth two in the bush" adage. "My price or no dice, and I'll pass this information on to someone else," she'd said. The promised supporting documents would be given to him after payment in full.

Using this information would mean taking on the DNC. He would have to threaten to expose their plot almost a year early, which would render it useless. Their plan was pretty ingenious, he had to admit. When the president's popularity had almost immediately gone south, instead of trying to appease people, he'd kept pushing and pushing his agenda on the American people. He and the Democratic Party had been able to accomplish more on their liberal agenda than ever before. Everyone started saying "Courtney would have been better" referring to Courtney Christopher, his close runner-up for the Democratic nomination in the last election's primary. The plan was to use his unpopularity to make her popular, in essence setting up his runner-up to step in at the last minute and capture the nomination. The Republican nominee was weak. He was beating the president, but he wouldn't stand a chance against Courtney. She had spent the last three years on a self-aggrandizing goodwill tour around America. Everyone assumed she was hoping for a vice-presidential nomination.

If he could get the DNC to agree to use him as her running mate, as the vice-presidential candidate in return for his silence, he could ride Courtney's popularity train right into the oval office. He could run for president the next term or the one after, depending on how long she held office. Of course, he would have to change parties again. This time he was better known. Well, even Ronald Reagan had done that. He would just say he had come to the realization that the citizens he represented agreed with the platform of the Democrats rather than the Republicans. It was all political double talk anyway. Who cared which party he represented?

But take on the DNC... could he do it? He was in favor with them right now. Dalton pulled out his phone. He might be a little unpopular with the DNC for a while, but it was worth it for the vice-presidency. He punched in Tiffany's number.

"I'm in. When do we meet?"

Jay jogged the rest of the way home in the rain, unlocked his condo, and went for an old towel to dry off his dog that stood dripping in the entryway. "You're a good sport, Riley," he said soothingly as he dried the dog's thick, short coat. Riley hadn't seemed to mind the rain, and he sat contentedly while Jay rubbed him dry. After Jay was done, Riley rearranged his bed and went to sleep.

After Jay's side trip to return Madison's key, he was soaked too. He dropped the towel next to the washing machine, dried himself off with another one, and changed clothes once again. "I'm going to have to do an extra load of laundry if I run into Madison any more times today."

He was starving, so he grabbed his wallet and keys. It had stopped raining again, so Jay decided to walk to a restaurant nearby for Cajun food. "A little jambalaya would be good," he decided. After he ate, he could run over to Max's to see if he was available for a pickup game.

As he walked, he thought back to the last couple of times he'd run into Madison. She'd seemed different. She didn't babble on, but that wasn't the only thing different about her. He couldn't pinpoint exactly what had changed. Well, she looked different. Her hair was a mess, she was sopping wet, and a little dirty. Maybe that was what made him realize for the first time how vulnerable she was. His thoughts went back to her conversation with her boss that he'd overheard. Now there was someone from whom Madison needed protection.

Madison was such a long, formal-sounding name. Jay thought it didn't fit her. He ordered his food and paid for it with cash. He'd started using his credit card only for emergencies after he discovered that people, without meaning to, spend a lot more when using plastic instead of cash.

While he carried his food to the park that had been his destination earlier and sat on a bench, he wondered if Madison had a nickname. "Maddie..." he tried out. That sounded like a name for a pooch; his next-door neighbor had a dog named Maddie. "Mad," he decided on, enjoying his spicy jambalaya.

Jay didn't think Mad and her boss were dating. "Hero worship," he decided. She was probably impressed with the senator's position. Jay had done some investigating and had learned the senator was something of a womanizer, but maybe Mad hadn't heard the rumors. In his late thirties, Stanfield was an imposing figure, taller than average. He enjoyed the finer things in life, often on the taxpayer's dime. He was a user, a turncoat. Jay hoped he was using only Mad's speechwriting abilities.

Suddenly it occurred to Jay that his article might make trouble for Mad. He hadn't thought about the repercussions to her job. What would happen when his story came out in tomorrow's paper?

Tiffany arrived at the George Mason Memorial more than a few minutes early. She'd overestimated how long it would take to walk from her car. She'd parked far enough away to avoid drawing attention to her meeting with Dalton. She was sure every lot had cameras.

As she approached, she hoped the senator wouldn't be late. She eschewed sitting on the dirty bench as birds visiting the memorial had left behind their calling card. Pretending to read the inscription, she glanced around. There were not many tourists at this spot, just as she had expected. The rain had stopped, fortunately.

When she spotted the senator, she took a deep breath and pulled farther into the trees. He walked straight to her without looking around. His confidence that they would not be seen and recognized was either impressive or foolhardy. Either way, it was a fine line.

Tiffany opened her purse and handed the senator a large manila envelope. Dalton reached inside his suit coat and produced a smaller one. The exchange happened without a word. She tucked her envelope in her purse and surreptitiously counted the bills. He'd brought large bills as she had requested, so the count didn't take long. As previously agreed, they parted immediately. No one seemed to notice them. Tiffany walked in the other direction from where she had parked. She would take the long way around.

She looked over the Potomac as she walked, watching two people canoe past her. They pulled their paddles out of the water and floated along, taking a breather.

Life is a river, too. It would keep flowing along whether or not you got on and rode, and it would take you where it would if you didn't paddle. She knew farther on there was whitewater; which direction, she wasn't sure. Were they heading toward rough water? It was hard to imagine as she watched the lazy canoe.

Maddie had enjoyed a leisurely bath, the warm water almost putting her to sleep again. When they first arrived home, Franky had gotten another bath, too, which he hadn't enjoyed quite as much as she was enjoying hers. She didn't want to put him through that again, but his muddy paws couldn't simply be wiped off this time. He was off pouting on the bed right now.

Cuddled in her fluffy robe, Maddie was enjoying another cup of hot chocolate as she studied the speech written earlier. She could be done with this rewrite in no time. She deleted the long part about the future programs. "This speech was too long before, anyway. He wanted time to meet the people afterward." It occurred to her that the senator hadn't said that. He'd said, "The people will want to meet me afterward." Maddie thought that was an odd way to put it, arrogant even. Was that what he meant? No, he must have just misspoken.

It didn't take long to pad the speech with the quotes of famous people as Dalton requested. Maddie had minored in history and was somewhat of an expert on some of these figures. "Done," she sang as she closed her laptop.

She flicked on the TV and a lamp, not wanting to watch TV in complete darkness. *Born Yesterday* was just about to come on. Maddie had seen *Mr. Smith Goes to Washington* last week. It was fun to watch movies that took place in the city she lived and worked in, although it was 60-70 years or so since they had been filmed.

With no intention of setting foot out of her apartment before her appointment with Dalton tomorrow, Maddie quickly made a cheese omelet for her supper and popped a bag of popcorn to enjoy with her movie. She settled in on her couch with her plate of food, ready to travel back in time to Washington circa 1950. Franky must have smelled her food because he joined her on the couch.

"You've got a bowl of dog food in the kitchen to eat. I've noticed you've put on a pound or two. We'll get out and walk more, but you're going to have to cut out the people food, too." Franky sat next to her looking expectant until her omelet was gone. He sniffed her bag of popcorn and looked at her hopefully.

Maddie ignored him. At one point during the movie, she exclaimed, "What a ditz!" when the main character, Billie, said something particularly naïve. For the most part, she watched the movie in silence as she usually did. When it was over, she yawned, ready to go to bed. It wasn't very late, but this had been such an exhausting day. In addition, she hadn't had anywhere near the amount of coffee she usually drank.

Maddie thought about the movie, as she got ready for bed. Billie, the character played by Judy Holiday, was very ignorant of politics in the beginning. She studied and in the end, she'd learned a thing or two about it and turned the tables on her abusive boyfriend and his dirty political dealings.

Maddie decided there were similarities between them. Although she wasn't nearly as naïve as Judy Holiday's character was at the beginning of the movie, she'd had to learn the way Washington worked when she'd started as a speechwriter for the senator. She still had a lot to learn. She hadn't been paying much attention to current events while getting her degrees.

Maddie took Franky out for the last time before turning in. The sky had cleared; the stars were visible. Glad the rain was over, she wasn't sure what tomorrow would hold, other than a meeting with Dalton, but it had to be better than today.

Jay walked up the stairs to Max's apartment, not sure what he'd find. Maybe he should have called first before driving over. The last time he'd been there, Max had tried to straighten up a little, kicking a couple of pop cans and food bags under the couch to join the balls of dust Jay could already see were ready to roll out. Jay had tried to relax, but it was the clippings of toenails on the coffee table that turned his stomach. It was an adventure every time a closet door was opened whether a baseball, a winter glove, or a hockey stick would come tumbling out. Once Jay was sure he'd seen a mouse in the kitchen, peeking out from under the pantry door.

He knocked, but Max didn't answer. Maybe it was just as well. Jay preferred having his friend stop by his place. He headed back to his car, pulling out his phone. He hit Max's number but didn't get an answer. Shrugging, he gave up and drove home. He could just as well turn in early.

"Tiff!" Tiffany stiffened hearing a man call her name. No, not her name, *her nickname,* which no one called her in this city, except her sister, Kate. Had she been followed? She turned slowly.

It couldn't be him. It just couldn't be. Why would Mitch Peters be walking along the Potomac? Why would Mitch Peters be in Washington D.C.? She couldn't breathe.

Mitch seemed to have no trouble breathing. He ran up, grabbed her in a hug, and twirled her around. Then he kissed her. And it wasn't one like you'd give an old friend. It mirrored their goodbye kiss seven years ago when she left for college and never returned. A long kiss goodbye.

He was laughing; he looked so happy to see her. All she could think was why was he here? He didn't belong in her life anymore.

Seven

Friday, Maddie woke up before the alarm went off. This allowed her to enjoy a few extra minutes lying in bed before nudging Franky. He definitely wasn't ready to get up, so she headed toward the kitchen alone, started her coffee, and took her Bible outside to her balcony. Her chaise lounge, which barely fit on the small balcony, was soaked. Maddie hung the cushion over the black rod iron railing to dry and went back inside. A steaming cup of coffee with a generous splash of cream, and she was ready to read. She sat on the couch snuggled up with her afghan, reading and enjoying the morning.

Her great-grandmother had knitted the afghan before she was born. Maddie had studied the design many times. She'd pondered how, unknowingly, an ancestor she'd never known had passed something tangible on to her, a descendant her great-grandmother would never know. Maddie thought of writing as the same sort of passing along, but it was being done now, in the present. If she could help people understand something, touch them, or teach them with her writing, even if she never met the readers, she'd passed along a piece of herself. She closed her Bible and said the same prayer she'd prayed since deciding to pursue writing as her career, "Lord, use me in whatever way You choose, but please use me."

Maddie made herself a breakfast burrito and was munching on it at the small dining room table when Franky wandered into the room and sat down next to her, looking hungry. "Oh sure, now you get up when food is involved." Franky looked so appealing, she considered giving him a bite of eggs. She decided against it. She knew she wouldn't be helping him lose the weight he'd gained.

"Sorry, boy, dog food's in the kitchen." Franky ignored the hint. "Ah, waiting to see if I'll drop something on the floor, eh? Nope." Maddie picked up her plate and quickly washed it and put it away.

She headed to her bedroom to get ready. Might as well wear her favorite blue suit, since she'd barely worn it yesterday. She'd found herself thinking about Cute Guy this morning. "I wonder what he does for a living." He looked pretty fit. Maybe he worked in the fitness industry as a personal trainer or something like that.

Pulling her skirt off the hanger, she was appalled to see a coffee stain! "I looked this suit over twice yesterday to make sure there wasn't anything spilled on it! I've got to get this to the cleaners." She hurriedly put on a pair of black tweed slacks and a gray silk blouse, finished getting ready as fast as she could, and took Franky out. She grabbed her satchel, purse, and stained suit and got in her car. Fortunately, the dry cleaner was just around the corner.

By the time she finally found a parking place, she'd convinced herself the suit was probably ruined. The stain must be set since it hadn't been treated promptly. Despite her high, high heels, she ran into the shop and got in line behind the only customer in the shop, a man who had a jacket slung over his shoulder. Maddie knew that jacket.

"I've got this!" she exclaimed in an almost triumphant manner, waving her wallet as if she were the highest bidder at an auction. Jay turned around looking not very surprised, but the woman behind the counter seemed slightly shocked at her outburst. "I stained it; I'm paying for it," she explained as she pulled out her credit card. "Also, I've got a stained skirt from the same accident. Do you think this coffee stain will come out from this fabric?" Tucking her claim slip into her purse, Maddie smiled at Cute Guy. She almost said, "We've got to stop meeting like this!" but she was afraid he would agree with her.

Tiffany sat at her kitchen table cupping her latte in her hand again to protect it from her cat. Ebony hovered nearby waiting for Tiffany to let her guard down, something Tiffany never did.

Except with Mitch, she did let her guard down, came the nagging thought. That was the whole problem. When she got home last night after running into him, she'd gone straight to her bedroom and pulled out *the letter* from its place in an old scrapbook at the bottom of her closet. It was the last letter, the last communication she'd had from him at all. The only one she'd saved. She hadn't read it since the one time the day it arrived.

She fingered it now. Did she want to dredge that up? She slid it from its envelope remembering his bold, careless handwriting, which was nothing like her precise script. She hesitated before finally unfolding it.

As she read it, a wave of emotion came over her. He loved her; that was obvious from the letter. She slid it back into the envelope.

Her doorbell rang. She dabbed at her eyes carefully with a napkin and pulled out her compact to check her makeup. Tiffany didn't tear up - ever. She certainly didn't cry. She didn't even bother to buy waterproof mascara.

She looked at the time, annoyed at the interruption to her routine. Dropping by Tiffany's without calling first was not acceptable. Bringing her latte with her for safekeeping, she opened the door.

Her sister, Kate, was standing outside her apartment with a grin on her face. Would that girl never grow up?

"I just happened to be in the neighborhood...," she said.

Tiffany took a sip of her latte as she moved aside to let Kate enter.

"Oh, a latte! I want one. Make me a latte, Tiff."

"Don't you have to go to school?" she said. Kate had followed her to D.C. and was a freshman at Georgetown University.

"Yes, but I have time for my favorite sister to make me some coffee," she said brightly. She headed for the kitchen, passing through the tasteful living room. The art deco theme was spread throughout the apartment.

Tiffany raised one eyebrow. "Why do you always say that? I'm your only sister." Tiffany poured the milk into a pitcher and expertly frothed it.

"You're still my favorite," she smiled as she sat down at the table and picked up the letter.

Tiffany smoothly took the envelope out of Kate's hand, but not before she could read who the sender was.

"Have you heard from Mitch, Tiff?"

"This is an old letter," she said as she put it in her purse and continued preparing the latte. Evasiveness came as naturally to her as breathing.

"Reading old love letters? You're still in love with him. I've always known you two were meant to be. It's fate. It's destiny."

Tiffany wasn't willing to put her life into the hands of something as fickle as fate. "Mom shouldn't have read you so many fairy tales. Real life is not 'happily ever after.'"

"Maybe it's not 'may the best man win' either," said Kate.

"No, it's 'may the best woman win,'" Tiffany said handing the drink to her sister in a to-go mug. "And I want that mug back."

Jay smiled but shook his head. No way was he letting Mad pay. "As generous as your offer is, I always promised my mother I wouldn't let a woman pay my dry cleaning bill."

She wasn't letting it go. "But your mother didn't count on your meeting me!"

He had to agree with her there. "Neither did I." Jay was surprised to find he was glad he had met her. He wasn't too sure the feeling would be mutual after her boss read Jay's article that came out today. She seemed too cheerful, right now, so she must not know anything yet. Should he give her a head's up?

"Look, Mad, let me take you out for breakfast."

"Breakfast?" Her phone rang. She fumbled around in her purse looking for it. "I'd love to, but I have an appointment I have to go to." She looked a little confused at his offer and distractedly answered the phone, "Hello?"

Jay could hear Senator Stanfield's voice through the phone. Mad pulled it away from her ear and started to move away. Jay reached out and touched her arm. "I don't understand, Senator. Article...what article? Yes, I was on my way. Okay. Bye."

Mad seemed preoccupied with her phone conversation. She hung up and started for her car. Jay grabbed her arm. "Wait! Let's get a cup of coffee," he said almost desperately.

Mad turned and looked at him. "*Coffee*? You want to get *coffee* with me?"

Jay didn't drop her arm. He'd heard enough of her conversation to know that she was about to be hurt, maybe even fired, and it was his fault. He'd never meant to harm her in any way. He hadn't thought about the consequences of what he'd done until it was too late. He couldn't let her walk into that meeting unprepared.

"Yeah, The Daily Grind is just up the street..." Seeing her face, he backpedaled and pointed in the other direction. "...or Starbucks. Starbucks would be good."

Still distracted, Mad started walking toward

her car again. "I'll have to take a rain check. I've got an appointment right now." She called out as she was closing her door, "Thank you, though," and quickly drove away not noticing they hadn't exchanged contact information.

Well, he'd tried. It was small consolation. Maybe she was better off the way she was, anyway. She had her innocence going for her. Jay wasn't usually the type to go after a story at the expense of all involved. At the end of the day, he still wanted to be a man of integrity. He shook his head. What had he done?

Dalton hung up the phone and started pacing back and forth in his office. What had that woman just done to his career? He picked up the paper again, quickly reading through the article. It had to be Madison who leaked the information to that busybody Jay Clark. Jeanie was the only other person who had been in his office, and Madison had already taken the list of programs with her. Anyway, Jeanie was too dumb to know how to leak information. Madison was just clueless enough. Or was she? Maybe it was an act.

But what to do about it? Should he fire her? He didn't want her taking revenge on him. If she had leaked it purposely, she might have more dirt on him that she would use against him. If she did it accidentally, did he want someone so incompetent working for him? Of course, her naivety had come in handy before. He had been hoping it would come in handy in a different way. He grimaced. Was it worth keeping her around hoping that someday she would give in to his advances? He hadn't tried anything yet.

He decided the only thing he could do was question her about the article and see if she told him anything. If she didn't, he'd just stay out of the spotlight and wait to see what happened with public opinion. In light of the information Tiffany had given him yesterday, bad publicity at this time was the last thing he needed. He hadn't even had a chance to contact anyone at the DNC yet, and now he'd have to wait until this died down before he could. His faux pas wouldn't win him any popularity contests with the DNC right now. Dalton had never liked complications. He would make sure anyone who crossed him would wish to God they hadn't.

He got out his cell phone. He needed to meet with someone before Madison arrived, someone a little more accustomed to smoothing out complications like this.

Relaxing in the shade of the patio at Le Pain Quotidien, Tiffany bit into a cheese almond Danish. She ate what she liked and for the privilege took exercise classes regularly. She sipped a mocha and tried to enjoy the delicious food and gourmet coffee, but thoughts of Mitch and their chance meeting the night before were all she could concentrate on.

It had been so hard to drive away from him that day seven years ago, her car overloaded with the stuff she was taking to college, her heart full of the pain of saying goodbye. But she'd been strong.

She'd shut that door, locked it, and buried the key when she left her small hometown of Tekoa, Washington for university. Through the years, when Kate still lived at home and tried to catch her up on what was going on in Mitch's life, Tiffany had stopped her cold. "That's all water under the bridge," she would say coolly.

But now the water had flowed back upstream. She and Mitch had exchanged business cards. He was in town for a job interview with some humanitarian organization. A job interview! So he might be moving here! She closed her eyes and tried to breathe slowly. He couldn't; he just couldn't.

Tiffany was always honest with herself. He was the only man she'd ever loved. The only one she'd let close to her. She never let men in, never let them use her, thinking too much of herself to do that. Tiffany used them. She couldn't give up control over her life, over her destiny, to someone else. Couldn't and wouldn't.

Mitch had talked her into having dinner with him tonight. She wouldn't go. She had to keep control of her emotions. If she saw him again, would she be strong enough to say goodbye for good this time?

Eight

Maddie was very surprised at the offers from the Man with no Name. First, he wouldn't let her pay for cleaning his jacket. She'd won that one, though. "Or did I?" Maddie wondered aloud as she drove to her appointment. She'd been in such a hurry; she hadn't noticed who had paid for it. Next, he offered to buy her breakfast, then coffee. He seemed to want to talk to her. She didn't think he could be interested in her romantically. "Could he?" she said aloud, wondering. No, she was sure he couldn't be after the impression she'd given him. However, if he wanted to ask her out... but wouldn't he have to be very desperate to ask her for a date after those three horrible encounters yesterday?

Maddie's phone rang. "Hi, Liz."

"Are you driving?"

"What do you think?" Maddie slowed down to take the corner.

"I don't like to talk to you while you're driving."

"Okay, bye!"

"No, wait! Can't you pull over to the side of the road?"

"No, I can't. I'm on my way in to see my boss. By the way, I've run into Cute Guy several times."

"Literally?"

"You know, you're right, I really shouldn't be on my cell while I'm driving..."

"Spill!" Lizette interrupted.

"Actually, that's what I did. I spilled burning hot coffee on him."

"No!" Lizette sounded unbelieving.

"Yes, and later I ran into him again. I jumped into a bush when I saw him coming."

"Why would you do that?" Lizette said flatly.

"I thought he'd think I planned to run into him, so I tried to hide."

"Did you plan it?"

"No! Then he helped me get my hair untangled from the bush."

"Oh no! How embarrassing!"

"Then he showed up at my place with my key that I'd dropped in the bush."

"You haven't changed a bit. Stuff like that always happens to you!"

"It does not!" Maddie saw the light was changing to yellow and sped up, barely missing another car that started through the intersection when their light turned green.

"Remember at camp how you insisted on holding that boy's glasses while he went in wading? Then you broke them."

"I didn't do it on purpose! He should have warned me they didn't bend. Do you want to hear the rest of my story or not?"

"There's more?"

"I ran into him at the dry cleaner's today and offered to pay to get the coffee stain out of his jacket."

"That seems fair."

"He invited me to breakfast; then to coffee when he heard that I couldn't make it to breakfast.

He seemed sweet like he wanted to talk to me. Do you think he could be interested in me romantically after all that?"

"It takes all kinds."

"Liz!"

"Maybe he could see that even though you got off to a bad start that you are basically a wonderful person."

"Thank you."

"Just a little accident-prone."

"Gee thanks, well, I'm here, I've got to go. Bye." Maddie didn't wait for her sister's answering goodbye.

She parked and walked into the Hart Senate Building, went through security, through the impressive lobby. An elementary school must have been on a field trip. They milled around the giant sculpture paying no attention to their teacher who looked like she was getting frustrated. A couple of the children were playing hide and seek using the sculpture to hide behind. Maddie smiled at them and continued to the senator's suite of offices.

When she arrived, she checked in with Senator Stanfield's assistant, Jeanie. The senator had seemed in a big hurry to see her when he called, clearly upset about an article that had come out that had something to do with her. Yet he kept her waiting for nearly half an hour. She kept checking the time on her phone. He was usually so prompt.

Eventually, another man exited the office. Jeanie told her to go in.

Maddie picked up her satchel and purse and entered her boss's opulent office. She'd grown increasingly nervous sitting in the outer office waiting. She wasn't usually nervous around Dalton. Since this was her job, and she knew he didn't see her as anything but an employee, she was always able to maintain her professional composure.

Usually, they discussed the speeches she'd written for him over a table in the corner of the room. Today the senator didn't lead her to the more informal setting, but stayed in his chair behind the desk and motioned for her to take a seat in a huge, overstuffed chair in front of him. She perched nervously on the edge of it.

"Madison, let's get right to the point. How do you know Jay Clark?"

She couldn't be more confused. "I don't know any Jay Clark. Who is he?"

The senator paused, scrutinizing her face. "He's a journalist for the Washington Times. If you don't know him, where did he get the information for this article? You admitted to me yesterday you'd picked up from my desk the very list of programs he referenced in this story." He tossed an open newspaper across the desk.

Even before Maddie had a chance to read the title, "Senator linked to extreme fringe groups" she already didn't like the term "admitted." She started to get a sinking feeling as she silently read the article accusing Senator Stanfield of liaisons with several extreme left-wing organizations via the very programs she'd been ready to mention in his speech. "Those programs are left-wing?"

"Clark is twisting what he thinks are facts to

suit his purposes. He's a right-wing extremist who is always looking for ways to discredit me. For some reason, he has a personal vendetta against me, no doubt because I am a moderate."

Maddie was very confused. "All I can say is I don't know him, and I didn't tell him anything."

Senator Stanfield got up from his chair and walked around to the front of his desk. Perching on the edge and placing his fingertips together, he leaned forward, a position she suddenly found very threatening. She slowly leaned back in her chair.

"Madison, working for a senator involves a high degree of confidentiality. This was all explained to you when you were vetted. You were specifically instructed to employ security measures. Unfortunately, either you did not employ such measures, or..." the senator paused, stood up, and walked around to sit behind his desk again. "...or you leaked this information on purpose. So tell me, were you negligent, or did you leak it on purpose? How did this journalist get this list?"

Maddie shook her head. She was suddenly terribly weary from being falsely accused. "I don't know, but if he is 'twisting facts,' can't your press agent explain that?"

"Politics often seem easy to those who are unfamiliar with it, but it is more complicated than just calling a press conference and presenting your case. What I want from you is information on how all of this came about. Squelching false rumors may be an exercise in futility. This may die down if we ignore it."

Maddie was so upset with the accusations being directed at her by her boss, she was having trouble thinking. "Senator, all I know is that list never left my possession." Suddenly it was clear what had happened. "I did read the list over the phone at the coffee shop where I was waiting for you. Someone must have overheard it."

The senator nodded. "Yes, well, it seems that 'someone' was Jay Clark. How convenient for him that he happened to be near enough to overhear our conversation." He sat there for several minutes looking at her as if he expected her to say something. When she didn't, he continued, "In the future, please keep your voice down in public places when discussing state business. Do you have a printed copy of the speech I'm giving today at the university?"

Maddie managed an affirmation and handed him the copy she'd printed for them to go over together. The senator accepted it without looking at her.

"If you'll excuse me, I have a full schedule ahead of me," the senator reached for a pencil. She was clearly dismissed.

Shell-shocked, she grabbed her things and quietly left his office. She blinked several times when she stepped into the brilliant sunshine.

Confused, Maddie tried to remember where she had parked her car less than an hour ago. She wandered around the parking lot dazed until she found the car. Dropping into the seat, she laid her satchel and purse on the seat next to her.

She sat for a long while, still too dazed to

drive. She wasn't fired, was she? No. Reprimanded, yes, but there had been no mention of firing.

At the thought of the possibility of losing her job over this, all at once, her anger kicked in. She started her car, suddenly very eager to get a good look at Mr. Jay Clark, pulled out of the lot and accelerated. She could look him up online or drive to the Washington Times. The chances of him being there weren't good, though. He was probably out looking for his next prey. No doubt, he hung out in coffee shops all day waiting for people to blab secrets. He must have already been there when she spilled the coffee on that good-looking guy…

Maddie slammed on her brakes, and then quickly got off the main road before she could be rear-ended. Throwing the car in park, she remembered the senator's words, "How convenient for him that he happened to be near enough to overhear…" Maddie picked up her satchel and started digging around in it for the piece of paper she'd picked up from the floor of The Daily Grind. She found the yellow piece of paper, crumpled up, in the bottom of her case. It wasn't very big, but she could make out in a scrawled hand, a partial list of the programs she'd read aloud yesterday.

Maddie stared at the paper in disbelief. It couldn't be him. She couldn't accept that Jay Clark was the cute guy from the coffee shop that she'd run into, but here was the proof that it was he. Then she remembered he had called her "Mad" as if he'd already known her name, even though they hadn't introduced themselves yet. She felt victimized. He'd used her against her own boss.

She could have been fired, and he didn't care. All he cared about was his stupid story. Well, she hoped he could live with himself, the scandalmonger, going around ruining people's lives to promote his own agenda. "And he can pay for his own dry cleaning bill!" she said through clenched teeth, although she'd never checked the receipt to see who had paid it.

She just wanted to go home. She put her car in gear and drove as rapidly as the law would allow. Getting a speeding ticket would just make her week, and police were everywhere in D.C.

She slipped her key in the lock and was met by Franky. It seemed like years since she'd left him, just a couple of hours ago. She'd been in such a hurry to get her skirt cleaned. Maddie gave a short, bitter laugh. Strange how much difference a few hours can make. Then her biggest worry was a coffee stain. Now her job was in jeopardy, and if she were fired, who would hire someone who was a leak? Today she'd been used as a source to discredit her boss.

No, actually, she'd already leaked the story yesterday. She just didn't know it this morning when blithely waltzing through her morning ritual.

Maddie looked at the blank screen of her TV, remembering the movie she'd watched just the night before. "I guess I'm even more like Billie than I imagined," she thought wearily, dropping her satchel, purse, keys, and shoes in a pile by the door.

She plopped down in a heap on the couch. What should she do next? Confront Jay Clark? Look for another job? She needed advice and a shoulder to cry on, a non-furry one. She called her sister.

Lizette listened sympathetically to her tale of woe, inserting several "wow's" at just the right parts and an "ouch" or two. It was comforting to have someone who loved her sympathize with her. "What a rat!" was Lizette's comment when Maddie was done pouring out her story.

"What are you going to do?" Lizette asked.

"I don't know." Maddie wasn't ready to make plans. She was still in the venting stage.

Ever the practical one, Lizette was ready to give advice. "If I were you, I'd do a little investigating on my own. Find out what Senator Stand-field stands for."

"Stanfield," Maddie corrected automatically.

Lizette continued, ignoring the interruption. "I'm surprised you didn't do that before you agreed to work for him. If your boss is showing a genuine lack of integrity, do you want to work for him?"

"I want to be a speechwriter."

"Yes, but do you want to write speeches for a snake?" her sister asked pointedly.

Maddie felt the need to argue. "No, but in this economy, there aren't that many jobs out there, period, let alone good speechwriting jobs. He could have fired me today, and I never would have been able to work in this town again."

"Better to lose your job than to lose your self-respect. I know you. You couldn't be happy writing for a man with a forked tongue. I'm sorry, Maddie. I just noticed the time. I have to get ready for work.

Can we talk more later?"

"What are you, a Native American?"

"Native American? What are you talking about?"

"What are *you* talking about? You said 'man with forked tongue' like you were Native American."

"Maddie, stay with me here. I said your boss could be a snake. They have forked tongues. And I won't even go into how politically incorrect that statement was."

Maddie blinked. "Oh, yeah. That works, too. Well, I'll talk to you later." She felt very dull-witted, not able to keep up with her sister's quirky banter. They'd always had these quick exchanges when they were in high school. They'd shared a bedroom and would sit up giggling late into the night. Sometimes it would border on the ridiculous. Right now, though, she just felt tired.

She returned her phone to her purse. What was she going to do right now was the question. "More hot chocolate," she decided and went into her tiny kitchen.

Nine

Jay stood watching the spot where Maddie had driven away. He certainly had a dilemma on his hands. He walked toward The Daily Grind, but when he reached it, he couldn't go in. He headed toward Starbucks instead, and he called Max.

"Max, I think I got Mad in trouble."

"Are you surprised?"

"Now I can't bring myself to go into the Daily Grind."

"Scene of the crime?"

"I guess. My whole career, I've been dedicated to the truth."

"You're always saying 'The truth will set you free.'"

"And it does," Jay said.

"The truth is you used Mad."

Jay stopped walking and sighed. "The mainstream media lie. People need real facts to make sound decisions about their legislators."

"But you still used her," Max said

"Honestly, it didn't bother me that I was using her until I got to know her a little better. I just figured she was a ditz and deserved it. What's the matter with me?"

"You're just a little too ambitious. Did you try apologizing?"

"I tried to this morning when I ran into her at the dry cleaners."

"You sure have run into her a lot. What is that? Three times?

"Four. You're right, Max. I need to apologize right away. I've got to go." Jay hung up. When it was his turn in line, he ordered his usual, brewed. No fancy coffee drinks for him. While reaching for it, he suddenly knew what he would do.

Maddie had finished her hot chocolate and had just dozed off when she heard a knock. Stumbling to the door, she mumbled a sleepy, "Who is it?"

"It's Jay Clark," came back, muffled, through the door.

Maddie yanked open the door, instantly awake.

There he stood, on her very own steps, the enemy. What nerve! Normally, one would think self-preservation mode would have kicked in, and he'd have the good sense to stay away from her. "Back for more intel? Got a follow-up column to write?"

"No. I brought you a peace offering." Jay had been holding his arm behind him. He brought out a Starbucks cup from behind his back.

Maddie looked from the coffee to the eyes searching hers. He was looking at her with something that could only be called hope. "You brought me coffee? What is this, a joke?" She folded her arms across her chest making no move to accept the drink.

Jay shifted holding the cup closer, waving it a little under her nose. "No. I told you. It's a peace offering. Medium latte, extra hot," he said soothingly, resisting the urge to smile or stutter.

Maddie looked at him suspiciously. She

thought she saw his lips twitch. "Yeah, you're hilarious." She turned around, about to close the door.

"Wait!" Jay stuck his foot in the door. "C'mon, you've got to drink this. I've never had a latte in my life. I got it just for you."

Maddie still looked suspicious, "Like I would accept a gift from you. Not only are you A. a user..." she ticked the points on her fingers, "...but B. you've probably laced the coffee with sodium pentothal, and when I'm under its influence you'll be ready with your handy, little notepad, scribbling down my every word while I reveal all of my boss's secrets." She moved to close the door again, but his foot was still in the way.

Jay shook his head. "Sodium pentothal? What an imagination. Here, I'll drink out of it first as a gesture of good faith."

Maddie shook her head. "No way would I drink that after you did. Haven't you ever heard of a thing called germs? They're sneaky, evil, little beings that are often invisible. They blend in and infiltrate their surroundings in a seemingly innocent manner all dressed up incognito as something wonderful like coffee or as strange men who..." she stopped. If she finished her sentence, she would start crying.

"...trip you in coffee shops." Jay nodded. "Okay. Fine, forget the coffee." He set it on the porch railing. "Look, Mad, I came here with three things to say. First..." he ticked the points on his fingers, looking straight into her eyes, "I want to apologize. I am very, very sorry. I was so excited when I overheard what you said that I rushed home, wrote the article, and sent it off before I'd thought about how it would affect you." He waited.

"What's number two?" Maddie looked at him expectantly.

Jay looked confused, "Number two? What do you mean number two?"

Maddie explained, "Number one is typically followed by number two."

"We aren't done with number one, yet."

"I'm done with number one. I don't forgive you. What's number two?"

Immediately, Maddie could see her refusal to forgive wasn't what Jay had hoped would be the end result of "number one."

"I didn't mean to hurt you, Mad. I didn't think how it would affect your job," Jay said softly.

Maddie looked away, tears in her eyes. "Yeah, well, I walked into a routine meeting I'd scheduled with my boss to go over something, and was completely blindsided by accusations of being either a leak or painfully inept."

Jay nodded, "When I thought of it, I tried to warn you."

"'Let's have breakfast,' is not a warning. 'You are about to walk onto a land mine.' That is a warning!"

"I'm sorry I didn't warn you better."

"Apology not accepted. What's number two?"

Jay shrugged. "If you won't forgive me, then number two is out."

"What's number two?"

Jay mumbled looking away, "I was going to ask you out to dinner."

"What!" Maddie practically shrieked. Jay looked back, genuinely surprised. "I was just accused of leaking my boss's secrets to you, and now you want to be seen in public with me? Then I definitely will be fired!"

Maddie made a move to slam the heavy door. Jay stepped back, hands in the air, almost falling down the stairs. It was obvious she didn't care if any of his appendages were in the way.

Jay took out a pen and a business card and wrote, "Skip #2. If #1 happens, call me. There's a #3." He placed the card on the top of the Starbucks cup and left.

Maddie opened the door. "And another thing..." She stepped outside. He was nowhere to be seen. The only remnants of his appearance were the cup of coffee and his business card. Reading the card, she glanced around again to make sure he was gone. She shrugged, picked up the Starbucks cup, and took a long, satisfying drink. As she turned to walk back in Franky tripped her. She dropped the latte, splattering the entire porch. She sighed and went in for a bucket and rag.

Jay drove away deflated. "I saw that going another way," he said to himself in his rearview mirror. In fact, he'd been thinking of restaurant choices on the way to her house, wondering what kind of cuisine she liked.

She was right, though. She could hardly plead innocence if seen publicly with the man who had written a column disparaging her boss. "Of course, I was writing articles discrediting him long before Mad came to town." He wondered where she was from. Would he ever know even basic facts about her now that she hated him?

He drove home and let himself into his apartment. Riley met him at the door as usual. Jay changed clothes and snapped a leash on his dog. "We should go to the park. You didn't get much exercise yesterday with all the rain, and if we should happen to run into Mad out walking her dog…"

Jay warmed up then started at a fairly fast pace. He slowed down to a very slow jog when he reached Mad's place. She was nowhere around, although her car was in the driveway and some lights were on. He jogged to the park and went around it several times. She never showed. On the way home, he slowed down again when he came to her house, but he didn't see her.

He showered and changed back into his regular clothes. He knew he'd better check in with his boss and see what his next assignment was, but first, he'd need some lunch, "and another cup of coffee." He convinced himself he needed a pick-me-up and wasn't just looking for her. Well, he almost convinced himself.

She wasn't at Starbucks when he stopped in there, so he continued to the paper and his next assignment. Max called him as soon as Jay stepped out of the building.

"Hi, Max, what's up?"

"That's what I called to see. What's up with you? Did you ever apologize to Mad?"

"I tried. I even brought her a latte, but she wouldn't forgive me."

"That's tough. Want to get together?"

"Later, right now I'm writing a follow-up to my last column."

"Really? Wouldn't it better to let that rest a little?"

"My boss thought it would be good to get some reactions to it."

"It might be good for the paper, but not for you."

Jay was frustrated. "Does no one remember that I was doing exposes on Senator Stanfield long before Mad ever came to town?"

"Believe me, I remember. You read them all to me. Have you seen Mad since you tried to apologize?"

" A few days ago I ran into her everywhere I went. Now I can't run into her by accident no matter how hard I try. I'd better go. I have to get this done for tomorrow's edition. Maybe I'll run into her at the senate buildings."

Jay got off the phone. He kept his eyes open, as he interviewed whoever was left in town since Congress wasn't in session, but he didn't see a trace of   Mad.

Ten

Tiffany hesitated before entering the restaurant. What was she doing here? She refused to lie to herself. It was more than just meeting an old friend for dinner. She couldn't have stayed away if she tried. That was part of the reason for the 3,000-mile move. That and because she was uniquely suited for a career in the nation's capital. If she'd stayed in Washington state, she couldn't have broken up with Mitch, and she'd needed to end it. She should walk away, now, today. This relationship couldn't go anywhere. She entered the restaurant anyway.

The venue was her choice, and he'd agreed to meet Tiffany` there, rather than pick her up, without questioning her excuse that she wasn't sure where she'd be. It wasn't true. She wanted to have the autonomy to skip this meeting, to change her mind.

Mitch smiled and rose when she walked up to the table. He looked better than he had the night before when she bumped into him running along the Potomac in his jogging clothes. He wore a nice suit, and Tiffany knew nice when she saw it, and it looked tailor-made to fit him. He kissed her on the cheek and helped her with her chair. She'd always liked that about him. He was considerate of women, kind to his mother, always treating his little sister like a young lady.

"So, have you been back to Tekoa much?" Tiffany asked steering the conversation to a topic she considered safe.

"Oh sure. My folks still live there. You know, 'In Tekoa, you're always welcome.'"

"How could I forget? It's the town's motto. I think the mayor even put it on his tombstone," she said. Mitch laughed agreeing.

"I think I heard that," he said.

"How are Ashley and your parents?" she asked.

"Great, Ashley is in her junior year. She's attending UW."

"Like her brother," Tiffany smiled.

"Like her brother," agreed Mitch.

"She worshiped you," Tiffany said lightly. "What's she studying?"

"Pre-med. She wants to be a pediatrician."

Tiffany nodded. "She'll be a good one. "

"You missed the class reunion a couple of years ago," Mitch said.

"A five-year - did I miss much?" Tiffany laughed.

"Just about everyone showed up... except you."

"I couldn't get away. It was so busy," Tiffany said smoothly.

"Hmm, busy... with work?"

"Yes, with work," she said.

Mitch let it go. "And of course there is the Slippery Gulch Celebration. That always draws people back."

"The event of the year." Tiffany laughed.

"Remember the year you were crowned queen?"

"Was that the same year you did the dunking tank, and the whole town lined up and sunk you over and over?" Tiffany smiled.

"I think so. Good thing it was for charity," Mitch shook his head remembering.

"Didn't you ever wonder why everyone was such a good shot?" Tiffany grinned mischievously.

"What did you do?" Mitch raised one eyebrow.

"I got Jeremy Malone to fix the mechanism with a hair-trigger so every shot that even barely touched it dunked you." Tiffany laughed.

"Nice, and to think I spent all these years missing you."

Tiffany didn't say anything.

"Here's the spot where you say you missed me too... assuming you did," he continued when Tiffany didn't answer him.

"Of course I missed you," Tiffany said. She looked around for the waiter.

"You're more beautiful than I remember," Mitch said softly.

The man wasted no time, she'd give him that. Coming from anyone else, it might have sounded insincere, but he was as transparent as they come. He didn't take his eyes off her. Tiffany couldn't meet Mitch's eyes. This was not the place she wanted to go tonight. She should have figured it would be a romantic walk down memory lane.

"Thank you," she said. She concentrated on the menu. "So I suppose you couldn't find a job in Tekoa. Surely you haven't been out of work since you finished college?"

Mitch smiled. "No, not many jobs are available in Tekoa. I work in Spokane, though."

Tiffany kept her eyes on the menu. "So, how did the job interview go?"

"Great! I think it's in the bag. I meet with the board next week, Tuesday."

Tiffany looked up, startled. Why was she surprised? Smart, good-looking, and warm, he was wonderful with people. Who wouldn't want to hire Mitch? But he couldn't move here. He couldn't.

She closed her menu and ordered a salad when the waiter arrived, although she didn't know how she would eat it when it came. Tiffany was suddenly sick to her stomach.

Dalton threw the paper down in disgust. Jay Clark was out to get him. That was the only possible explanation. Clark had written several exposes in the past attempting to discredit him. The journalist had probably been following his speechwriter around ever since she'd started, to see if he could get any information out of her. Now on Saturday, here was another article Clark wrote interviewing any conservative he could squeeze a quote out of. Maybe it was time to bring in some help. He needed to know if Madison was leaking information, and he had to do something about Clark. Dalton crumpled up the newspaper and threw it in the wastebasket. He pulled out his cell phone. Time to set his plan in motion.

Saturday stretched out ahead of Jay with no real work to do. The Sunday edition was always short on real news articles, except for the items that came over the wire. The only features were the soft news that had been planned ahead of time. Most weekends, Jay had little maintenance to do at home, since he lived in a newer condo with no lawn mowing required of him. On this particular weekend, he had almost no writing projects to speak of either. He was planning another article on government spending, but he was finding it hard to concentrate. He couldn't help wondering if Mad had been fired, which was a very real possibility. There were many people Jay would like to see fired, including almost half of Congress, but Mad wasn't one of them.

After puttering around all day Saturday, Jay was glad when Max stopped by that evening. It allowed him to stop procrastinating on his article and instead lie around doing nothing. Jay hadn't seen or heard from Max since Thursday. Practically, the first words out of his mouth were, "Got a ten you're not using?"

Jay had never refused to loan a friend money and gave it to him readily, but why would Max, someone with a lucrative career as an IT guy, suddenly need to borrow money every time he came over? Jay meant to ask him but forgot because he wanted to tell him the rest of his encounters with Mad first.

Max headed for the kitchen. "Good call, Jay. She is a menace. You know some people just have bad luck follow them."

Jay frowned. "I don't believe in luck. You make your own luck."

"Accidents, then. Accidents follow her." Jay heard his refrigerator door open.

"Hey Max, speaking of accidents, it's your turn to drive tomorrow. Be on time when you pick me up," Jay called after him.

"Ha ha. Yeah. I meant to tell you, Jay. I'm going to visit a new church tomorrow."

"Really, which one?" Jay was surprised. Max had been going to the same church Jay did for years and had seemed pretty happy there.

"I forgot the name."

"Okay, where is it?"

Pause. "I forgot the address."

Jay walked into the kitchen. Max was bent over looking in the refrigerator. "Then how are you going to find it?"

Max closed the door. "Man there isn't anything to eat in there." He walked back to the living room, flopped on the couch, picked up the remote, and turned on the TV. "You want to go shoot some hoops?"

Jay had interviewed enough people to know when someone was avoiding a subject, but he knew Max would tell him if it was important, so Jay didn't press him. He took the remote from Max and turned off the TV. "Yeah, I've been cooped up in here all day. Let's play some basketball."

Tiffany had a raging headache all weekend. She didn't even need to lie when Mitch called to ask her to spend the day with him Saturday, and she had to refuse. She got off the phone immediately and went back to bed. It was caused by the stress of contemplating Mitch moving to her city. But what to do about it?

It wasn't an option not to answer his phone calls. She couldn't just ignore him, couldn't bear for him to think less of her. It was the reason she'd left Tekoa all those years ago. She realized even then what a career in politics would entail. He would try to be her conscience if she were in a relationship with him. It would all come out, her lies, her deceptions, the bribes. He didn't think she was a saint, but he had no idea what she was willing to do, short of selling herself, to accomplish her dreams.

Eleven

On Sunday morning, the sun came up. It had come up yesterday morning, too, just as it did every day, but Maddie hadn't risen with it. Right before noon, on Saturday, she'd decided lying in bed feeling sorry for herself all morning wasn't getting her anywhere. She got up, made coffee, and spent the afternoon lying on the living room couch feeling sorry for herself.

But Sunday was different. Sunday had a purpose that Saturday didn't have. Sunday had a place to go - church. Maddie could have lain around again, today, but there were three reasons she didn't. One, she didn't want to. She'd had enough of that yesterday. Two, if she didn't show up at church today, her friend, Chloe, would notice and would call to see if she were sick. And three, she wanted to go. She wanted to be involved in something bigger than herself and her problems. She wanted to stand in a group of people and worship God, the creator, who knew her and loved her.

Maddie showered and picked out her clothes, blue jeans and a light sweater. Even though it was warm and sunny outside, it was always cold in the warehouse-like building. When she first started going to New Life Worship Center, she'd dressed up as she always had when she'd attended the mainline denominations back home and in college. She'd quickly caught on that everyone at New Life dressed casually to put visitors at ease.

When she walked outside to her car, she paused to breathe in the fresh morning air and waved at a neighbor, Snowball's owner. Franky often chased Snowball, and Maddie knew the owner blamed her for that. Maddie hurried to her car when the woman ignored her.

Maddie wanted to arrive at church early enough to get a cup of coffee from the café in the foyer. They served Starbucks and put out a bowl for donations rather than charge people, another way to welcome visitors. Her friend Chloe saw her there.

"I got our seats, Maddie."

"Usual spot? I'll be right in."

As Maddie greeted a few people she knew and took her place next to Chloe in the auditorium, she knew she could relax. Finally, a place where she wouldn't be running into Jay Clark, either literally or figuratively. She wondered where he went to church. She'd assumed he was a Christian because he hadn't let loose with a string of expletives when she'd spilled hot coffee on him. On the other hand, he could be just a moral man who could control his tongue. Either way, she was glad he wasn't here. So why was she thinking about him?

The warehouse-like structure was unlike any church Maddie had ever attended. There were no stained glass windows at New Life. In fact, there weren't any windows at all, because there were several screens set up in the auditorium, and windows would cause a glare. New Life used technology in all its glory to reach out to a younger generation that might find traditional forms of worship slow-moving. Maddie liked it because the teaching was relevant and the worship was contemporary. Many of the songs she'd heard on the local contemporary Christian music station were played here every week.

After singing several worship songs that reminded Maddie that God wasn't called Almighty God for nothing and could be trusted as always, she felt more at peace than she had in several days. She didn't know the couple sitting next to her, so an introduction was in order. They seemed to want to get to know her better, and they chatted for a few minutes before the pastor began his message. Maddie spilled her coffee in the process of sitting down; Chloe gave her a package of tissues to mop it up. Maddie considered getting another cup, but being in the middle of a row it was hard to get out.

The pastor didn't use a podium. He carried his Bible around with him on the stage as he spoke. In the past, Maddie had heard many messages that she felt were just for her. Today was no exception. The message was on humility. The pastor pointed out that humility was not so much thinking of yourself as lowly, as not thinking of yourself more highly than you ought. "Everything you are, God made you to be. Not bothering to use the talent given to you by God isn't humility. It's laziness. Humility is recognizing the difference between the gift and the Giver of the gift. One is meant to be used and the other is meant to be worshipped. Don't get the two mixed up, and worship the gift or try to use the Giver." He went on to point out that just as Jesus, the greatest example of a servant, did not regard serving as subservience, but as true service, done in love, so also, everything we did for each other, no matter how lowly, was serving God. The pastor invited everyone to lay their gifts, their lives, on the altar to be used by God as He saw fit.

Maddie realized she had been looking at her gift, writing, as her primary way of service to God. When she'd been saying, "Please use me in whatever way You wish," what she'd meant was, "Please use me as a writer in whatever way You wish."

She truly wanted God to be in control of her life. "But I want to be a writer, too, God," she prayed as she stood at the altar. As she started to walk to her car after the service ended, she realized it all came down to trust again. "Every lesson begins and ends with faith," she thought as she reached her car. She didn't notice another car pulled out of the parking lot shortly after she did and followed her.

When Jay arrived home after church, Max's car was already sitting in his driveway. Whatever church he'd visited must have gotten out early.

Max jumped out of his car and ran over to Jay before he had his keys out of the ignition. "You will never guess who I met today!" Max said as soon as he'd opened Jay's car door for him.

"Let's see… You were at church. The Pope? Billy Graham?" Jay unlocked the door to his condo and motioned Max to go in first. Max motioned back for Jay to go in first. Riley came over, stood by Jay, and stared at Max.

"Oh brother. I didn't mean I wanted you to guess. I meant you really will never guess!"

But just as Max said that Jay knew. It was Madison.

"Madison McPherson," they said in unison. Max looked puzzled.

"Did you just say 'Madison...'?"

"McPherson," Jay finished and nodded.

"You don't seem surprised." Max looked disappointed. "I thought you'd be more excited."

"Max, you're going to think this is weird, but right when you said that, I knew. I've been thinking about her ever since I brought her that coffee, trying to figure out a way to see her again. Asking myself, 'What could I say to get her to forgive me?'"

Max dropped on the couch and folded his arms across his chest, looking skeptical. "Jay, there was nothing mystical about coming up with her name when you've been thinking about her nonstop. What happened to you? I thought you didn't like her. Three days ago, you didn't want anything to do with her. You called her 'a menace.'"

Jay tossed his car keys on the coffee table and sat on the couch. Nodding he said, "Yeah, that's because she spilled hot coffee on me. She's pretty, though, isn't she?"

Max looked mystified, "Make up your mind, man. She spilled coffee at church, too"

"So, you met her. What did she say? Did you mention me?"

Max frowned. "I just met her. You know, 'Hi,

I'm Max.' It was a coincidence. I just happened to sit next to her. Why would I mention you? I didn't want her to hate me. From what you've told me, you're dead meat."

"So you sat next to her? You should have invited her out after church for lunch."

"Then she would have thought I liked her. She went up to the altar afterward, anyway."

Jay looked thoughtful. "So what is the name of this church? Do they have a Sunday evening service?"

Max shook his head unbelievingly, "Really? Stalking a woman at church is not cool."

"But it's fine to stalk a woman somewhere else? Which commandment is that? 'Thou shalt not stalk at church'? Anyway, it's not stalking to accidentally show up at the same church at the same time."

"Yeah, well, you know where she lives, don't you?"

Jay looked away. He'd already told Max the story about bringing back her house key.

"Have you been by there too 'accidentally'?"

Jay didn't want to admit he had, and he wasn't willing to lie, so he still didn't say anything.

"Uh-huh. And since she works on Capitol Hill, and you're over there all the time, how easy is it to just run into her 'accidentally'?" Max started talking in a high-pitched voice, "Oh, Madison, fancy meeting you here at the Capitol building…"

Jay punched Max's arm "I would never say, 'fancy meeting you here' to anyone and you know it. And I don't talk in a girly voice!" He had to agree, though, that his behavior bordered on stalking, but he wasn't telling Max that or how he'd looked all over Capitol Hill for her including the senate building her boss worked in. "You want to get some lunch?"

Max stood up. "No, thanks. I just ate." He headed for the door.

Jay grinned. "That's never stopped you before." He looked away from Max and said nonchalantly. "So, what was the name of that church you visited this morning?"

Max shook his head. "I'm not telling you."

"Don't worry. I'm not going there. I just wondered."

Max opened the door. "Someone has to save you from yourself."

"Stop being so melodramatic. What's the name of the church?"

Max shook his head again. "Nope." Then he snapped his fingers. "Hey, I've got an idea. If you want to run into her 'accidentally' again, go hang out at that dry cleaner. She's such a klutz, she's probably in there several times a week, and I've heard it's a real hoppin' place. Then you could say..." Max minced around and used his high voice again. "Oh, Madison, I used to think you were a klutz, but I woke up yesterday, and decided you're so pretty that I've fallen love with you!" He puckered up his lips and acted like he was going to kiss an imaginary Madison.

Jay moved to punch Max on the arm again, but Max beat him through the door, quickly pulled it closed behind him, and ran out to his car.

Jay stopped with his hand on the doorknob. Come to think of it, he hadn't picked up his jacket yet... then he remembered the dry cleaner was closed on Sunday.

Maddie's phone rang as she was walking in the door. She dropped everything to answer it. Lizette's voice was welcome. It was nice to have a sister who would call just to see how you were doing, to make you feel better.

She wandered into the kitchen to make herself a sandwich while she talked to Liz.

"So how was church this morning, Maddie?"

"Good. I met some new people. One couple was pretty friendly. She's a little weird. She's into vampires." Maddie squirted spicy brown mustard on her bread.

"Oh, that's nice." Liz sounded distracted. Maddie guessed she was making lunch, too.

"Really? Nice? I think it's a little creepy. She's really into it." Maddie licked her fingers. "I realized something though."

"What's that?"

"While I've been saying "Use me as you see fit, Lord." What I meant was "Use me as a writer.""

"If you're careful not to let ambition get the upper hand, you'll be fine. What did Dad say about it?"

"I need to go, Liz."

"Gas stamps? What will that dictator think of next?" Lizette sounded frustrated again.

"Really? Is gas going to start being rationed?"

"Rationed? Where did you hear that?"

"Weren't stamps used to ration gas during World War II?"

"No. I mean yes, but they aren't rationing gas now. The president has decided poor people need a gas stamp program like the food stamp program."

"You're kidding! Who's going to pay for that?"

"Who do you think? It's called taxation. Maddie, you've got to pay more attention to current events."

"Well, right now, I need to pay more attention to my lunch. I'll talk to you later, Liz, arrivederci."

Maddie knew she needed to be more current. She'd start reading the paper and watch the news more and TCM less. After all, it looked like she had plenty   of   time.

Twelve

Tiffany's headache was gone by Monday, but her anxiety was mounting. Mitch would meet with the board tomorrow. She went to work, and although her mind was on her problem, her face did not betray her emotions. All of Tiffany's movements were small and controlled as usual. No one at the midmorning staff meeting could have guessed the level of frustration she was feeling.

She didn't leave the conference room immediately after the meeting ended. She wasn't brooding exactly, but she needed some space to think. Her boss, Senator Reed noticed and came back into the room, closing the door.

"What do you need?" he asked quietly as he sat down next to her. He always got right to the point. It was one of his charms, although to some people it could be unnerving. In his early 60s, the senator seemed like a warm, benevolent grandfather though he never hesitated to take out his opponent with whatever means necessary. He had been involved in politics for decades.

Tiffany considered. It was always give and take with the senator. If he was able to help, she'd owe him a favor. He was corrupt, but she knew him well enough to know that he wouldn't ask her to do anything she would have to refuse to do.

"I need someone to leave town," she said, matching his bluntness. "An old… friend is here for a job interview. I need this person to be passed over for the job."

"Sounds simple enough, with which corporation is he interviewing?" Her hesitation to identify which sex the friend was, was not lost on the senator, and he must have guessed it was an old boyfriend.

"It's a humanitarian organization. He's meeting with the board tomorrow."

As she gave the details, the senator nodded. "I'll make a call," he said.

She marveled at the ease with which he took care of things. He always knew someone from whom he could call in a favor or some way to make things happen. A sudden lightness came over her, knowing Mitch would be leaving in a day or two. She smiled. "Thank you."

Monday morning dawned with nothing for Maddie to do. Her boss hadn't given her the next assignment at their last meeting as he usually did. "What if there is no next assignment?" Maddie wondered aloud. By Monday evening, with no word from the senator, she could see she needed a plan. She couldn't just sit around like a lovesick teenager waiting for the phone to ring. Not that she was in love, not after that last meeting with the senator, but what was she going to do until she heard from him? "I'll give him a week before I start job hunting," she decided.

She made a list of everything she'd neglected since she'd been dedicating so much time to her work: clean the closets, walk the dog more, exercise, cook more healthy foods and eat less fast food and pizza, read those books she didn't have time to read before, call her sister more. When the week was up, then she would actively start looking for another job, although she wasn't quitting until her paycheck stopped being deposited automatically in her bank account. If he wanted to pay her for doing nothing, she'd take it. She hoped he would show her the courtesy to let her know if she was being fired rather than just stop paying her.

Maddie considered if she should quit, rather than wait to be fired, which would look bad. "So would quitting a job after three months," she reminded herself and decided to stick with the plan. She'd let him fire her if it should come to that.

Mitch called Tiffany right before he was to go in to meet with the board. She didn't take the call. He would want to hear encouraging words like he always handed out freely. She refused to go there. She wouldn't listen to the message he left, either. She didn't delete it, but she didn't listen to it.

He sent her a text message. "Pray for me!"

She knew it! A few of his comments the other night made her think he'd gotten religious. Well, that sealed the deal. No way someone religious would go along with political dirty dealings or want to be associated with someone who worked that way. If it hadn't been before, their relationship was history.

Mitch called again after the interview. Tiffany took the call that time. He sounded less than confident. "I don't know. It didn't go as well as I had hoped. I felt like I was being given the third degree rather than being interviewed for a job. It certainly didn't go as well as the first interview did, Tiffany."

"That's too bad, Mitch, but there must be a lot of jobs in Washington state."

There was silence on the other end of the phone. "I didn't come out here just for this job. I think you made a mistake when you left. No, you didn't make the mistake. I did when I didn't follow you. I still love you, Tiffany. I've never forgotten you."

Maddie saw, by following the news, that the senator made no appearances most of that week. She guessed he was letting the uproar die down before he put himself in the public eye again. In the past, he was usually in front of the camera several times a week at some dedication or community event for free publicity.

When the newest grocery store in the area was dedicated near the end of the week, she'd caught part of the grand opening ceremony on the local news. Senator Stanfield spoke briefly. It sounded like the speech he gave was reworked from the speech Maddie wrote for him to give at the university last Friday. "Except he took out all of the interesting parts and kept only the boring ones." She called her sister after the news story to discuss it. She felt a grim sense of satisfaction. "Ha! He's sunk to a new low, giving regurgitated speeches. And it wasn't good."

While watching the news footage, she thought

she saw Jay on the outskirts of the crowd taking notes. She couldn't help being a little bitter. "Doing a little honest journalism, huh Jay? Not sneaking around in coffee shops spying on people today?"

Her sister had been her support, encouraging her to pursue the things she'd been neglecting. "Don't focus on the senator or that newspaper guy. Don't look at this as if you're a victim. Live your life."

Maddie wasn't ready to ignore everything the senator was doing. In the next edition of Jay's paper, there was an article on the grocery store opening with a scant paragraph about the senator appearing. Maddie guessed whatever her boss said wasn't very newsworthy. She was sure that was exactly the effect he was going for.

Dalton clicked off the news. The store opening had gone just as he'd planned. He'd stripped just about everything but the bare bones from the speech he'd given at the university. The effect was less than appetizing to a crowd that was already wowed by the giant new supermarket. The senator grimaced. He was always stuck catering to the masses, many of whom couldn't think for themselves. He would've backed out completely, but he had obligations. If he canceled now, it would look like he was guilty as charged in that article of Jay Clark's. He'd briefly considered letting Jeanie write his speech for him, saying the opportunity to speak came at the last minute, and Maddie was busy or out of town. He was sure she would've come up with something equally boring, but he was afraid she would catch on to what he was doing. Nobody would notice he'd already given that speech anyway. All the people had cared about at the Grand Opening Day event was the sale price of their legal drug, coffee, anyway.

Jay hadn't given up looking for Mad everywhere he went, but he stopped expecting to see her. He'd finished the article on government spending. He spent most of his time working on his latest article. The topic was the benefits of requiring term limits for the legislative branch and the Supreme Court. He'd managed to finagle covering the opening of the grocery store when he heard Senator Stanfield was scheduled to make an appearance. He was hoping to find her, finally, but Mad was nowhere to be seen, and the speech made for a very dull story. The coffee shop inside the store was more interesting than the toned-down senator who gave one of the most boring speeches Jay had ever heard. People were drifting away while he was still speaking. The half-priced coffee offered inside the store might have played a part in dispersing the crowds, but only a small part.

Maddie had a very long, very boring time waiting for the senator to call, except for catching up on some of her reading. She crossed off a lot of items on her checklist and dropped a couple of pounds from all of the exercise and cleaning she did. It was hard to keep from contacting the senator to see if he had any writing for her to do. If there was anything she disliked more than conflict, it was unresolved conflict. She hated letting the accusations hang in the air. She wasn't sure if Senator Stanfield was shunning her to punish her like she was a naughty child, or if he simply didn't have any work for her to do since he was laying low. She felt off-balance, waiting for him to call.

When he finally did call, he was, as usual, short and to the point, always such a busy man, the senator. No time for pleasantries unless he was talking to the voters. He didn't mention the time he'd spent ignoring her or the leaked information. He simply told her to meet him at his office.

After their phone conversation when Mitch said his feelings hadn't changed, Tiffany had made an excuse to hang up, but not before agreeing to meet him soon for dinner. All of her planning had garnered nothing. Mitch wasn't leaving; he was still looking for a job in the area, and now she owed her boss a favor.

Dalton thought of something he had to do and got off the phone with Madison as quickly as he could. He raced out of his office, barely taking the time to tell Jeanie that he'd be right back. Unbelievably, he'd completely forgotten to pick up that ridiculous message from last week until just now when he remembered it while he was talking to Madison.

When he reread the email message, he realized he had been instructed to answer it right away, but his answer had to be left in another secret spot. All of this ridiculous spy nonsense was making him late for another meeting. He slapped surgical tape to the base of the Washington Monument and headed back to his office. Couldn't they come up with something more original than tape stuck on a slab of marble?

As he traveled, he realized he'd been in such a hurry he'd forgotten to hide the printout of a decoded email on the table in his office. He didn't need to worry about Jeanie reading it. Since she was unable to read and follow simple instructions that were handed to her, she certainly wouldn't go looking for work. But Madison was on her way there. He hurried, but he knew he wouldn't beat her. He hoped for her sake that she didn't read the message. He wasn't ready to take drastic measures with her, yet. He was still considering who to approach on the DNC and how to go about it, and he might have a way to use Madison in his plan "as bait for a trap" he whispered to himself.

Thirteen

Maddie arrived twenty minutes early for her appointment. Jeanie smiled and said, "I haven't seen you around here lately. The senator was called away on an urgent matter, but I expect him to return shortly." It was obvious Jeanie didn't know how far Maddie had fallen from favor. She told Maddie she could wait in the senator's office.

Maddie laid her satchel on the table where she and the senator usually worked. His laptop was already open. Maddie pulled hers out, opened it, and sat down. Wondering what her next speech would be about, Maddie looked at the notes that were lying next to the open laptop. A cramped scrawl was written above some typed print. It was difficult to read, but Maddie could just make out "Jobs bill...close...too obvious if you vote with us... better abstain."

She suddenly realized this wasn't notes for a speech, and what she was reading wasn't meant for her eyes. She grabbed her laptop, stuffed it in her satchel as fast as she could, and ran over to sit on the couch. She pulled out her phone and tried to compose herself, pretending to be checking her messages. Almost immediately, Senator Stanfield hurried into his office.

Maddie's heart was thumping so loud and fast she was sure Jeanie could hear it in the outer office, and she could feel how red her face was with the sudden exertion. Had he seen her? She noticed the senator seemed out of breath, and quickly put the papers that had been lying on the table in a drawer in his desk. She could feel him looking at her, so she took a deep breath, closed her phone, and carefully put it in her purse. Trying to act normal, she looked up and smiled saying, in what she hoped sounded like her normal, pleasant voice. "I guess I'm a little early."

The senator seemed to be sizing her up. Maddie refused to look away or show any emotion. She'd done nothing wrong, wasn't trying to pry into affairs that weren't her own. She'd stumbled on the information by mistake.

Senator Stanfield cleared his throat and walked over to the couch carrying a manila folder that had been sitting on his desk. Quickly, he went over some ideas he had for his next speech to be given to a community group Wednesday night. There was nothing newsworthy about anything he touched on. He wanted the speech to be even shorter than usual, with no witticisms, anecdotes, or quotes.

If she didn't know the senator was trying to escape the public eye, she would have said something about the poor quality of the subject matter and the banality of the presentation. As it was, this ridiculous speech was simply trivial. Why even give it? Why not just cancel the event? She'd always believed in excellence; to write something of this caliber felt wrong. She had a hard time not telling the senator so.

It was petty of her to focus on the inane speech in light of the cryptic message she'd stumbled on. "But really! This insults their intelligence!" A group of seniors subjected to this should nod off with no trouble. She would if forced to sit through it.

Dalton wasn't sure what to think. Madison acted as if she hadn't read the paper, but he couldn't be sure. She seemed so innocent, but it could be an act. If she were working with that crafty Jay Clark, he wouldn't be surprised at anything she did.

Dalton was hoping that soon he'd be able to use the information Tiffany had given him. He was thinking of contacting Darrell Washburn, who basically ran the Democratic party himself. Dalton wanted to do it with a little finesse, though, perhaps entice the Democrats to approach him.

He'd been having Madison followed, but that hadn't turned up anything. She'd spent all of her time in her apartment. He was ready to give her another chance at writing speeches, but now that she'd had access to sensitive information again… He knew he shouldn't have left that where she could see it, but he'd been in such a hurry to answer the email that he hadn't taken the necessary precautions. Well, he couldn't do anything about it now.

Maddie exited the building a little slower than her usual quick, purposeful step. In case anyone was watching, she didn't want to give the impression she was in a hurry to get out of there. She could hardly contain herself, though, as she got in her car, keeping up the slow pace for a necessary few blocks. She hit the gas as soon as she was out of sight of the building.

She wouldn't have believed it if someone else had told her, but she had seen the proof for herself. Senator Stanfield was going to absent himself purposely so he wouldn't have to vote on the Jobs bill, to help the Democrats pass it over the Republican vote. How could he do that to his constituency? Maddie had seen on the news this week how slim the margin of votes was, and how inflated the bill was. Despite its name, it wouldn't create jobs, but merely hand more money to government agencies to waste, "or to line pockets," Maddie said grimly, convinced she knew whose pocket would be the first to be lined.

What to do with the information? Even if she knew which watchdog group to contact, there was no proof. She wasn't going to sit on this information, though. Just as it had for Billie in *Born Yesterday*, the time had come for Maddie to no longer let ignorance be her excuse.

She drove home quickly and let Franky out while she paced around in the yard. "I need a plan." Franky pricked up his ears when he heard her voice and wagged his tail. Maddie studied her small dog. "How right you are Franky. We should go for a walk."

Maddie changed clothes and grabbed a leash. She and Franky took off for the park. Some guys were playing Frisbee with a couple of really big dogs, but Jay and his German shepherd weren't among them. Maddie walked her small dog around the park over and over until Franky started jumping up and swatting her on her leg, a sure sign he was exhausted. She ended up carrying him home. As she walked, she studied each house she passed. She was pretty sure Jay Clark must live in her neighborhood. She'd run into him too many times for it to be a coincidence unless he was stalking her. "No, I'm the one who came off as a stalker," she reminded herself. Franky thought she was talking to him and licked her chin. Finally, she gave up. "Why didn't I just google him?" she asked herself. Then she remembered she still had his business card. Should she call him? What could she say? "I've finally decided to forgive you,"? But she hadn't forgiven him. She just needed him. But first, she needed more information.

Fourteen

Tiffany again chose the restaurant where she and Mitch would meet. This time she made sure to pick one that wouldn't be missed if bad memories were created that evening. They had reservations for La Maison Belle, which was supposed to have very good food but wasn't a place that she frequented. Before she met Mitch tonight, she needed to decide how to tell him that they couldn't be a couple ever again.

She left work early to go home to change. She mounted her apartment stairs to the second floor and moved along the outside balcony, greeting her next-door neighbor that worked the nightshift. Their paths rarely crossed as Tiffany typically returned home when the woman had already left for work. Tiffany knew little about her neighbor except she liked quiet during the day to sleep.

Tiffany dropped her keys in her purse on the table by the front door. Ebony stretched but didn't get up from her place on the couch. Tiffany went straight to her closet to choose something to wear. There was that new dress; it still had the tags on it, a midnight blue satin. She would look amazing. But did she want to look amazing tonight? She held it up to herself in front of her mirror. If she wore the dress tonight, she would never wear it again. She hung it back up and pulled out a red number that had been worn many times.

Ebony joined her from the living room while she sat at her vanity table to freshen her makeup.

When she turned on the light, the cat rubbed against her leg. She stroked her head and then got to work applying her mascara. As she leaned forward, she stopped with the wand in midair, looking at the mirror, knowing what she'd say to Mitch tonight. He deserved nothing less than the truth. She'd lied to him too much.

Maddie put Franky down as soon as she walked through the door. "You might weigh only fourteen or fifteen pounds, but it adds up. You're supposed to be a miniature dachshund." Franky lapped up some water in the kitchen and returned to fall asleep in his favorite spot on the couch.

She thought about what her sister had said and pulled out her laptop. She googled her boss's name. She wasn't surprised how many times he was mentioned. He had been a senator for many years, and he was involved simultaneously in several projects. She found many articles that Jay Clark had written about the senator, but he wasn't the only person out there questioning if the conservative stance the senator claimed he had, lined up with his actual voting record.

What did surprise her were the rumors that the senator was thinking of running for president. She hadn't heard a whisper of that. "You'd think he'd tell his speechwriter what his plans were. Unless... there was a reason he was keeping it a secret," she said to her sister the next time she called.

Lizette agreed. "I told you he's a snake. I'm not too impressed with most politicians anyway. I'd keep a sharp eye on the journalist, too. 'Keep your friends close and your enemies closer."

"I'm hoping he'll be an ally, Lizette."

"The only person I'd trust less than a politician in Washington D.C. is a journalist, but it's a close second."

"Maybe I should quit. My boss is mixed up in some stuff he shouldn't be…"

"Well, aren't all politicians? Maybe you could get Dad's take on it."

Maddie started rubbing the phone over the couch while speaking into it. "Liz, we've got a terrible connection! Bye!"

Maddie, of course, knew her sister's opinion on politicians and had to agree with her in many cases. That didn't stop her from wanting to be a speechwriter, but perhaps she didn't need to work for this particular politician.

She delved into the senator's past. There was a lot of material to read. She couldn't possibly read it all. She skimmed article after article.

He had started as a Democrat running as a state representative but switched over to the Republican Party by the time he ran for his U.S. Senate seat. He'd told her that bit of background when he hired her, but the reason he'd given her at the time was that he'd had a change in ideology. From what she garnered on the internet, he'd kept most of his liberal viewpoints intact when he switched sides, contrary to what he'd told her.

She studied his voting record. From what she could see, when his vote didn't count, when there was a high Republican margin, he voted with them. When the vote would be close, though, he either voted with the Democrats or was absent. Jay Clark had raised many questions in the articles and editorials he wrote, but from what she read, neither he nor the others who questioned the senator's ethics were being taken seriously.

Now that she'd done her homework, Maddie knew it was time to get more information, the kind she couldn't get on the Internet. And she knew right where to get it.

Jay's phone rang. He looked at the screen but didn't recognize the number. "This is Jay," he said.

There was a long pause, and he almost hung up. "This is Jay," he repeated.

"This is Maddie," came the voice he'd been hoping for more than a week to hear again. He juggled and then almost dropped his phone.

"I'm so glad you called, Mad," he said.

"Yes, well, I didn't know anyone else to call." She said almost instantly, "I'm sorry. I didn't mean to sound quite that ungracious. Could we meet?"

He remembered what she'd said about being seen with him in public. "Sure, Mad. You pick the place."

"Can you come over here to my apartment again? I assume you must live in this neighborhood, right? So it shouldn't be a long walk."

"Walk? You want me to walk over?"

"Yeah, don't drive your car. I don't want it to be seen in my driveway. And come after dark."

Jay thought of joking about how his car wasn't that ugly, but he could tell she wasn't in a joking mood. "Okay, Mad. I'll be over as soon as it gets dark."

She hung up without saying goodbye. It sounded like he was the only one looking forward to this meeting. Her voice had been filled with what he could describe only as dread.

Tiffany heard a crunch. Ebony streaked into the living room and started meowing. Tiffany joined her to see what had upset the cat so much.

Ebony was perched on the back of the couch hissing and spitting. Tiffany didn't see anything out of order, except the cat's favorite toy was in pieces on the floor.

"What's the matter, girl?" she soothed, reaching out to pet the cat.

Ebony snarled and leaped into the air toward her. Tiffany instinctively jumped out of the way and spun around to watch the cat land. As she turned, she saw a man dressed in black with dark hair coming toward her! The cat clung to his head, scratching at the intruder's face. Ebony hung on, hissing and meowing as the intruder clawed at his face. He pulled the cat off and flung her aside

Tiffany lurched for the door, grabbing her purse as she passed it on the table near the entrance. She jerked the door open and raced down the outside walkway. The man followed her out the door, but once exposed, he hesitated; and then he ran in the opposite direction. Tiffany didn't stop running until she reached her car, got in, and roared out of the parking lot. While she was driving, she called 9-1-1 to report the intruder.

When she was a safe distance away, she pulled over, shaking, still talking to the dispatcher, and tried to calm herself. She looked in every direction to make sure she hadn't been followed. She agreed to return to her apartment after D.C. police arrived and waited on the line until the dispatcher gave her the okay to return.

Jay saved Mad's number in his phone and jogged over as soon as the sun set. It was starting to rain. He hoped he wouldn't have to run home in a downpour. He wasn't sure why she wanted him to come. Since he didn't know what to bring, he didn't bring anything. He took the steps two at a time and knocked quietly on the door. A dog started barking. She opened it right away as if she were waiting by the door for his knock. The small dachshund growled.

"Cozy," he commented upon entering. "Where are Sneezy and Dopey?"

Mad frowned and raised her eyebrows. Then she must have recognized that he was referring to the cottage shared by Snow White and the seven dwarfs. She looked around and nodded. "Yeah, it's small."

The dog had been following him around, growling low in his throat since the door had opened. "Hush, Franky!" Mad said. The dog stopped growling but sniffed Jay's shoes.

It was very small compared to his apartment, with ceilings that sloped so much he could barely stand up straight even in the middle of the room. He took a seat on the couch right away so he wouldn't have to worry about bumping his head on the light fixtures. The miniature dachshund scrambled up on the cushion next to him and advanced, still sniffing him. Jay liked dogs, so he petted him. "I forgot your dog's name, Mad." The dog must have found him acceptable. He licked his hand.

"Franky," she said sitting in a faded wingback chair next to the window.

"Franky," he repeated. "Is that a family name?"

Mad had to laugh. "No, it's short for Frankfurter. You know, he's a wiener dog. Get it?"

Jay felt stupid. That was pretty obvious. Why hadn't he thought of that?

He looked at her sitting across from him in her chair, just about as far away from him as she could get in the tiny room. She'd invited him here, but she wasn't saying anything. She certainly didn't seem out to impress him. He got the distinct impression that her goal was the exact opposite. Every time he'd seen her at the Daily Grind, her look had said that she cared about her appearance. Now, her hair was pulled up in a loose ponytail, and she was wearing baggy sweat pants and a T-shirt that was so faded he couldn't read what was printed on it, just University of Something.

He wanted to apologize again, but he thought they'd already covered that, so he sat silently waiting for her to say something. She leaned back in her chair, biting her lip. Suddenly, it seemed like something occurred to her. "Why do you keep calling me Mad?"

He guessed he'd been a little forward, giving her a nickname when he didn't even know her. "I'm sorry. Madison seemed so formal. What do people usually call you?"

"Maddie. Most people call me Maddie."

Suddenly there was a flash of lightning and all the lights in the apartment went out. Maddie screamed.

Jay spoke softly and calmly. "It's okay, Maddie. The storm knocked your electricity out. Don't worry. I'm sure it'll come right back on." He was right, but when the lights flickered and went back out a few minutes later, Maddie had disappeared.

"M-Maddie?" Jay stammered and his voice squeaked. Where did she go? She must have been very frightened; she'd obviously panicked when the power went out from the sound of that scream. How weird that she was in this very room a minute ago. Then he came to his senses. She had to be around here somewhere. Jay knew what to do. "Franky! Where are you, boy?" The dog would've followed Mad. All he had to do was find the dog. He thought he heard him whimper off to the left. He moved quickly toward what he assumed must be the kitchen and felt a sudden blow to his head.

The next thing he knew the lights were back on, and he was lying on the living room floor with Franky licking him on the lips. Mad was hovering over him with a bag of frozen peas and rooting around in his hair, obviously looking for a lump so she could administer the icy bag.

Jay tried to sit up, but he felt sick to his stomach. He laid back down.

"What happened? Who hit me?" he said.

Mad was still trying to find the lump. She was tenacious, he'd give her that.

"Here," Jay took the bag of peas from her and pressed it on top where his head hurt the most. He closed his eyes.

Mad sat back and studied him. She shook her head. "No one hit you. I think you tried to walk through the doorway and didn't quite make it. You're tall."

Jay opened his eyes. "I know I'm tall. You disappeared when the lights went out. I could tell you were terrified. I didn't notice the doorway was so low, because I was looking for you, and I could barely see."

Mad looked puzzled. "Terrified? What do you mean?"

Jay said softly, not wanting to embarrass her, "You screamed..."

Mad shook her head, "I didn't scream. I yelled. I stepped on Franky's bone!"

Jay looked confused. "Franky's...?"

"Bone," She finished, holding up the offending gnawed-on bone. "It's sharp on this end where he chewed it."

"So you're not afraid of the dark?"

She smiled. "What am I, seven?"

"But you disappeared..."

Mad stood up. "I went to find a flashlight. I would have told you what I was doing, but you were so busy trying to calm me down, I couldn't

136

get a word in edgewise."

Jay started to stand up. Mad looked worried but tried to help him. "Do you think you should get up so soon? I don't want you to faint again."

"I'm a guy,' said Jay sinking onto the couch. "Guys don't faint. I was knocked out."

She smiled, "You knocked yourself out," she said.

Jay nodded. "We writers have to choose the exact words to say what we mean. Don't we?"

Mad sat next to him on the couch, watching a little anxiously, clearly still expecting him to keel over at any moment. "Would you like something to drink?"

"Sure. What've you got?" Mad went into the kitchen and opened the refrigerator. Franky jumped up on the couch and settled down next to him.

"Not much. Do you want some orange juice? How about some hot chocolate or tea? It's a little late in the day for coffee."

Jay turned the bag over. "Hot chocolate sounds good. Could you bring me something to wrap around this? My hand is freezing."

She brought him a dishtowel with a lighthouse on it and went back to the kitchen. Jay wrapped the towel around the bag of peas and pressed it to his head again. "Maybe we should discuss why you asked me to come over," he called to the kitchen.

Mad came to the doorway. With her standing there, he could see how he could have conked himself on the head. She cleared it with only a few inches, and she couldn't be more than 5'4". The doorway framed her like a portrait, a casual portrait, but a portrait nonetheless. "I'm not quite sure. I came across some information today, and I didn't know what to do with it." She went back into the kitchen.

"What information?"

Mad appeared in the doorway with two mugs. She placed one on a coaster in front of Jay. He handed her the peas. "I think I'm done with these, thank you."

After putting them back in the freezer, Mad returned with a spray can of whipped cream. She held it over his cup with a questioning look.

"Oh yes," said Jay. Mad sprayed a generous helping in the cups, put the whipped cream away, and returned to join Jay on the couch.

Jay took a sip of the hot chocolate. "Okay, what information did you...? He drank more. "This is really good. What kind of mix is it?"

Mad smiled. "Mix? I mixed milk with cocoa powder and sugar." She took a drink. "And a little cream," she added.

"Wow... gourmet hot chocolate," Jay drank again.

Mad studied him. "You're not what I thought you were."

Jay felt they could be getting into dangerous territory here. Things were going so well. They were talking and having really good hot chocolate. Why bring up a time in the past when he almost got her fired? She was looking at him expectantly, but he didn't know what she wanted. He paused in indecision before asking, "Who did you think I was?"

She hesitated. "At first I thought you were someone who happened to be in the wrong place at the wrong time… again and again."

"At first?"

"Well, after I found out you wrote that article, I thought you'd set me up."

Jay set his mug on the coffee table. "That's not what you think anymore?"

"No. Now I'm beginning to think you were in the right place at the right time. I've read some articles you've written. You seemed to care about all of this," and she gestured with a sweeping motion.

Jay looked around at the small apartment, "All of what?"

Mad weighed her words. "You care about all of us, 'we the people,' who are so easily duped by the politicians who hide their lies behind complicated lingo. They call bad good and good bad. Being conservative and having old-fashioned values is 'extreme.' That kind of thing. I think that Someone Else orchestrated these meetings."

Jay wasn't sure what she meant but continued in the same vein. "You said you had some information."

Mad held up one finger. "First, what is three?"

Jay was confused again. It was a good thing Mad was a writer rather than a speaker. That way she could go back and fill in the missing information she kept leaving out when she talked. "I don't know. You tell me. What is three?" He held up one finger as she had.

Mad pulled out his card. "I see you've forgotten the note you wrote on the back of your business card." She read aloud, "'Forget number two. If number one happens, call me. There's a number three.'"

Jay was suddenly hopeful. "Number one happened? Does that mean you've forgiven me?"

Mad stood up and walked to the window. She didn't say anything, and Jay was suddenly nervous. He wished he could see her face.

Maddie couldn't look at him, just stood there with her back to him, weighing how much she could trust him. She barely knew him. Forgive him? She hadn't before reading on the Internet all of the articles he'd written. After reviewing them, though, his words had struck her as so sincere. That was the one word she would use to describe him, sincere. He was the same way in person.

Conversely, the senator had always struck her as a little too smooth, a little too quick with a compliment to be considered sincere. She'd always told herself that was part of being a politician. It was a persona he took on, not the "real Dalton," but she'd never liked being "handled" by smooth talkers and salesmen types, and she appreciated honesty.

She turned back around and took a deep breath. She knew she was going out on a limb. "I do forgive you. What you did, you did without thinking. Just like I read off that list of programs without thinking of the consequences of revealing my boss's agenda in a public place."

Maddie could see Jay was relieved. He picked up his mug and settled into some pillows.

Maddie returned to the couch, picked up her barely warm hot chocolate, and drained the mug anyway. "So what is number three?"

Now it was Jay's turn to hesitate; he seemed unsure of her reaction. "I think we should work together to expose your boss."

Maddie nodded. "I've come to the same conclusion."

She could see she had surprised him. "You might not be so surprised when you hear what I've discovered." She proceeded to tell him what she had read in Senator Stanfield's office.

"Jobs bill... close... too obvious if you vote with us... better abstain," Jay repeated. "Too bad you couldn't have gotten a copy of that piece of paper. That's pretty incriminating evidence against the senator."

"And against whoever sent the email, although it looked like it was in code, and he decoded it," added Maddie. "Senator Stanfield immediately put it in his desk drawer. I don't know if he locks his desk, but I can't very well go back to his office and rifle through his things. Can I?"

Jay shook his head and grimaced. "No, that's too dangerous in more ways than one. I don't know if the 'good senator' would physically harm you, or more probably would hire someone to do it. If you were caught, not only would that be the end of your job with him, but also you'd be committing career suicide."

Jay stood up and started to pace back and

forth, but he quickly ran out of room. Maddie guessed he was afraid of hitting his head again because when he reached the couch, he sat down. Although it had nothing to do with the discussion at hand, she couldn't help but wonder what his place looked like. It probably had high ceilings.

Jay looked at her seriously. "Okay, here's what we know. We know the senator started his political career as a Democrat and early on switched to the Republican side. It appears his switch was in name only. If he's still working for the Democrat party, they're probably financing him in some way. Maybe there is a paper trail in his financial record."

Maddie frowned. "Would he leave that lying around?"

Jay smiled, "Well, of course, it could be digital, paper trail is just a term, but I meant his bank statements would show he has large sums of money going through his account. That is something that would probably be subpoenaed if he were ever charged with something. He could have an offshore or Swiss bank account where he's hiding it, though. He's probably too smart to leave something like a bank statement lying around. Of course, he left that piece of paper out on a table where you or his assistant could see it."

Maddie shook her head. "I doubt if he normally does that. He must have been called away suddenly. I don't see what can be done, besides my going back to see if I can find that piece of paper or some other evidence."

"No!" Jay's reply was so forceful it shocked her. "Absolutely not! You are not going to do that.

It's too dangerous." He grabbed her arm. "If something happened to you because of an article I wrote..." he trailed off and must have realized he shouldn't have grabbed her arm because he dropped it and moved away from her on the couch. "I'd never forgive myself if anything else happened to you because of me..." he paused as if realizing he'd gotten too personal, "or if I hurt anyone else," he added quickly.

"Okay," she said slowly. "Then what are we going   to   do?"

Fifteen

When Tiffany returned to her place, there were several police cruisers in the parking lot. She breathed deeply, trying to restore her composure before approaching her apartment.

When she walked inside and identified herself, immediately she noticed her cat was nowhere in sight. She moved throughout her apartment, looking for the feline. "Ebony!" she called repeatedly. "Gone," she whispered.

"Who is Ebony?" the officer asked.

Tiffany dropped onto a caramel leather art deco sofa. "My cat," she said.

"Ms. Roberts, we need you to tell us about the intruder. It looks like the back door was forced."

Wearily, Tiffany began to describe what had happened. She realized in the middle of her story that she needed to contact Mitch and cancel their date. She sent a quick text explaining what had happened.

The police had her look around to see if anything was missing. Nothing seemed to be gone except Ebony. Maybe she had bolted in the melee. Tiffany's copy of the information she'd given to Dalton was in a safety deposit box at a bank in Virginia. She realized recovering those documents could have been the motive behind the break-in, but she didn't mention it to the police.

Jay surprised himself with how strongly he had reacted to Mad's brash announcement that she

144

might sneak back into the senator's office, but he had never been more serious. Maybe she's watched too many crime dramas on TV, he decided. How could she suggest such a thing? He had a feeling Senator Stanfield could be a very dangerous enemy.

Jay looked at Mad now, sitting on her couch, looking vulnerable again. She didn't need elegant clothes to look pretty, or need any makeup, he decided. She must not be wearing any makeup today. She had a natural beauty that didn't need to be hidden under cosmetics. He wondered why women spent so much time on those things.

Jay took a deep breath, "Okay, I'm going out on a limb, here, but I noticed earlier you said, 'Someone Else' orchestrated our meetings. I am assuming you meant that God has had a hand in all of this." Jay looked straight into her eyes.

Mad nodded. "I do. Starting with the coffee shop incident, if you examine the events, you'll see what I mean. What if you had gone to Starbucks last Thursday morning instead of going to the Daily Grind? What if you'd arrived half an hour earlier or later?"

Jay couldn't help but finish the thought in his mind, "What if we'd never met?" but he was afraid to say it aloud. What if it meant more to him than it did to her? He was already dreading when it would be time to say, "goodbye" and he wouldn't have a reason to run into her again. But wasn't that the way he had felt all along? Or at least since he'd returned her key to her when she had first looked so vulnerable. Every time he walked or drove away, he thought he'd never see her again, but he had. He was already sure Someone Else had a hand in his life before he met Mad. He'd known his whole life that God personally knew him, cared for him, and was watching over him.

"I think we should pray about it," Jay said. "We don't know what to do, but we both think something should be done, and that we were brought together to do it. Shouldn't we pray?"

Maddie agreed, bowing her head and closing her eyes as she always did. She didn't see him take her hands in his, but she felt it. His warm hands were strong around her small, soft ones. He began, "Precious Father, we come to You today to ask You to lead us. We don't know what we should do, Father, but You do. Watch over Maddie; keep her from harm, and help her not to do anything foolish. Amen."

"Amen," Maddie opened her eyes, "And thanks for that by the way!"

"You're a writer, not a spy!" Jay said, smiling as he moved toward the door. He stepped out onto the landing. He ducked when the eaves troughs dripped on him. "Your gutters are full."

Maddie stepped outside, too. "You're right; they're overflowing. I'd better do something about that."

Jay leaned back and looked at the roof. "That's a pretty steep slope for you," he said.

"How would it be for my 90-year old landlady, then?" said Maddie.

"Is *she* a klutz?"

146

"What? You think I'm a klutz?" Maddie asked.

"Who? You? Never." Maddie couldn't see Jay's face, but she didn't need to.   She could hear the teasing in his voice.

"Yeah, thanks for that, too." She watched as Jay jogged off, and she went inside. She locked the door and leaned on it smiling. She'd noticed when he took her hands to pray that there were calluses on them. She wondered if they were caused by working out. He certainly looked like he did. Her thoughts were so distracting and confusing. In the beginning, she thought he was just another good-looking guy. Then she was sure he'd never want anything to do with her because of her gaffes. Then he'd seemed to warm up to her, asking her out for coffee and breakfast. When she'd found out he'd used her, she didn't want to see him again. After he'd apologized to her, and she'd found out where he stood on important matters, she was back to liking him again. This time, though, it was because of who he was inside, a genuinely likable guy, who cared about people. When he had echoed her thoughts about going out on a limb, she realized how much of life was spent taking chances like this, how trust between people was required for any relationship to develop or continue.

She noticed he'd called her Mad again, though. Maybe he subconsciously thought she was crazy. Maddie frowned as she dropped onto the sofa. Franky jumped on her lap and started licking her face. She laughed. "I'm okay now, Franky. You don't have to try to make me feel better." She went to get ready for bed.

Mitch arrived as the police were wrapping things up. "How are you doing? Did he hurt you?" he said grabbing Tiffany in a hug as soon as he walked in.

She had to admit; it felt good to have him there. "How did you know where I live?" she asked.

"Kate," he said. She nodded. Of course. "She wants you to call her. She's worried about you. I canceled our reservations at La Maison Belle, too. So, tell me what happened."

Tiffany related the story again, skipping the part about the confidential information she'd leaked to Dalton. She'd decided that couldn't have been the motive for the break-in. Dalton hadn't even used the information yet. Unless somehow the DNC had found out that she had accessed the information, but she didn't see how they could have.

The police officer who had questioned her came over. "We're done here, Ms. Roberts."

Tiffany thanked him, and he and the other officers left.

"My cat is missing. I have to look for her," Tiffany said. She stepped outside and began calling Ebony. Mitch helped her, looking in the bushes.

"She likes to be up high. She'd more likely be in a tree," she said. They searched the trees around the apartment building, but Ebony didn't appear.

"I have an idea," Tiffany said. They went back into the apartment, leaving the doors open, and she made a latte. She took her time frothing the milk, but unfortunately, no cat appeared.

"Do you like lattes?" she asked.

"I do," Mitch smiled. Tiffany gave him the first one she'd made and began to froth more milk. Almost immediately, Ebony appeared and jumped up on the counter.

"Ebony!" she cried. Unmindful of her dress, she picked up the cat, which tried to worm free to get to the pitcher of milk. Tiffany was tempted to let her have the whole pitcher, she was so happy to see Ebony, but she knew it would make the cat sick. Instead, she poured some of the slightly warmed, frothed milk into a bowl and set it on the floor.

"Do you still feel like getting a bite to eat?" Mitch asked.

"I'm exhausted. How about tomorrow?" she asked.

He hesitated. "Tiff, you could stay with me, if you don't feel safe here," he said.

But Tiffany had other plans. "I'll be fine," she said.

"I'll call you," he said and kissed the tip of her nose.

As soon as he left, she closed and locked both doors and packed herself a bag. She could stay at a hotel, but she would feel too exposed. She knew that often the best place to hide was in plain sight. She called an intern she worked with but knew only slightly.

"McKenzie, I need a favor."

Sixteen

The next morning Maddie awakened to the sound of scraping. "Frank, stop scratching at the door. I'll let you out." Franky poked his head out from under the covers. "If that noise isn't you... then what is it?" Maddie sleepily crawled out of bed, grabbed her robe, and went to find the source of the sound.

Opening her front door, she almost knocked over a stepladder that was set up on her porch. Perched on it with a bucket and a garden trowel in his hand, was Jay, who was scraping leaves and gunk out of her eaves troughs. He was up to his elbows in goop, and let out a grunt of frustration, but managed to keep from falling as Maddie quickly reached to steady the ladder she'd run into. Unfortunately, Jay couldn't hold on to the bucket of goop and maintain his perch. Maddie nimbly dodged the bucket, but Franky who had followed her out to the porch wasn't quite so nimble. He yelped in surprise as the bucket landed upside down on him covering him with slimy gunk. Then he crawled out from underneath the bucket and streaked down the stairs toward the street.

"Franky! Stop! Come here, boy. Franky! Oh, Jay, stop him before he runs into the street!" Maddie frantically called.

Jay chased down the narrow, steep stairs after the panicked dog. Franky dodged all of his efforts to grab him until Jay caught up with him just before they reached the street. He dove for Franky, barely grabbing onto his hind legs. Sliding on some loose gravel, Jay scraped himself on the driveway. He came back to Maddie carrying the messy, wriggling dog. Both of them were covered with greenish-brown slime, and both of Jay's hands and forearms were scraped and covered with blood mixed with gravel.

Maddie reached out to take Franky, but Jay held him out of her reach. "No sense in you getting covered in this too. Which way to the tub?"

At the word, "tub" Franky started wriggling and almost fell out of Jay's hands.

Holding up the hem of her nightgown and robe, Maddie ran up the stairs, stepping carefully around the puddle of slime and into her small apartment. Jay followed her, ducking in all the right places until he entered her impossibly small, brilliantly pink bathroom. He gestured toward the tub. "Wow. Tiny. Even a dwarf couldn't stretch out in there."

Maddie obviously couldn't hear what he said over the running water, so he deposited the small dog in the tub and left. Maddie started scrubbing Franky again. "These last couple of weeks, young man, you've been both the dirtiest and the cleanest you've ever been."

A few minutes later, when she came out of the bathroom carrying the dachshund wrapped up in a towel, twisting and turning and trying to break free, Maddie found she was all alone again. She was about to head to the kitchen to make her morning coffee when she heard the now-familiar scraping sound. She put Franky in his cage with a dish of water and his dog food and went to the front door again. Carefully opening the door, she saw the slime-covered Jay back in his place scraping more leaves out of her gutter. She leaned back and shaded her eyes from the early morning sun.

When Jay saw her, he shifted a little on the ladder and overemphasized grabbing onto the overhang as though Maddie would topple him again.

"So funny. You know that could have happened to anyone."

"And yet it happened to you."

"I thought you went home to change."

Jay kept working and called down good-naturedly, "I figured why change with a certain girl and her dog in the vicinity."

Maddie didn't know whether to thank him for cleaning out her eaves trough or to be insulted by the comment. She crossed her arms. "Franky and I are not usually so klutzy."

"Say it isn't me that's bringing out this new side of you two," Jay begged.

Maddie laughed. "I'm afraid it is. It's sweet of you to do this. You know, that's a very dangerous place to be, on a stepladder at the top of these steep stairs."

Jay nodded and looked around. "I was nearly scalded to death the other day in a coffee shop. I like to live on the edge."

Maddie laughed again. "How about I make some breakfast?"

"That's your definition of life on the edge? Is

your cooking that bad?"

Maddie swatted at Jay and the ladder swayed. Jay grabbed onto the overhang in earnest to keep himself and the ladder from falling over.

"Sorry." Maddie bit her lip to keep from laughing.

"I'm sure you are." Jay studied Maddie; then he gestured to himself and the ladder tilted a little. He grabbed onto the overhang again. "I don't think I'm dressed for it."

Maddie headed back into the house. "Go change. I'll make breakfast."

"Okay, Mom."

"Besides, you shouldn't be standing around on my porch in broad daylight."

"That's true," Jay climbed down the ladder and jogged off.

Maddie tried to go back into her apartment, but she was locked out! As she went down the stairs to the rock garden, it occurred to her that she still had her pajamas and robe on. She started crawling around looking for her rock with the spare key in it. A shadow fell on her. Jay was standing there, shaking his head. She looked up and smiled, pulling her key out of the fake rock. Jay laughed and jogged off.

Maddie unlocked the door, returned the key to its hiding place, and let the still-damp Franky out of his cage. He tore around the apartment rubbing himself all over everything again. "You get more exercise out of a bath than any dog I know," she called after him.

She went into her room to pick out something

to wear. Franky came into the room to watch her select an outfit.

"It's only breakfast," she told him. Franky yawned and flopped down on the bed and went to sleep.

"You're right; I was talking to myself. What am I going to wear, though? Something fetching."

Franky jumped off the bed and brought his ball over to her. He dropped it at her feet.

"What? Oh, I didn't say 'fetch;' I said I should wear something fetching.' You need to improve your vocabulary, dog." Franky pushed the ball closer to her. Nothing seemed to look like she wasn't being obvious, so Maddie gave up and chose a bright pink T-shirt that was a particularly good color for her and some jean capris. She changed, applied some makeup, and went into the kitchen.

She pulled her cell phone out of her purse and called Jay's number. She held her phone with her shoulder while she measured out twice the amount of water she usually used to make coffee. She could hear the shower in the background when he answered. "Jay, what would you like for breakfast?"

There was a hesitation on the other end of the phone. She teased, "What? Afraid I'll poison you? I told you last night that I've forgiven you."

Jay laughed. "No, I just don't want to put you to a lot of trouble."

Maddie assured him, "It's no trouble. I like to cook, but it's no fun cooking for just myself. Besides, I have to pay you back for cleaning out my eaves troughs."

Jay said, "If that's why you're doing it, we might as well cancel. I've already decided it would be easier for you to move than to clean those particular gutters. When was the last time your landlord cleaned them out?"

Maddie squinted as she measured coffee beans into the grinder. "My guess is during Watergate. My landlady is 90 years old and weighs about 100 pounds. Can you see someone like that perched on top of that shaky ladder?"

Jay laughed, "Maybe she should just replace the gutters. Hey, make anything you want. I like everything...except squid - too chewy."

"Are you sure? I have some squid in the refrigerator that I just caught. It's still fresh," she said in a light, playful tone.

"Well, my favorite would be caramel pecan rolls."

Maddie nodded her head. "Agreed. No squid on the menu for breakfast today. It would take several hours to whip up caramel pecan rolls from scratch. But if you want to stop at the store and pick up some refrigerated rolls when you come back, I'll make them. They don't take any time at all. I'll use my imagination for the rest of breakfast. Bye."

By the time Jay got into the shower, the mud and gunk were dried and hard to get off. He had to soften it, standing in the hot spray for a while before he could scrub it off.

After he had dressed, he was in his car and on

155

the way to the store in no time. Parking was not a problem for once, and he walked into the grocery store behind a young girl and a guy with red hair. Jay tapped the man on the shoulder, "Fancy meeting you here," he said in a high-pitched voice.

Jay thought for a second that Max wasn't going to turn around. Only after the girl he was with turned with her eyebrows raised and a questioning look on her face did Max turn around, too.

Max's face was as red as his hair. Jay couldn't decide if his friend was embarrassed because of the girl or because of him. He didn't seem in too big of a hurry to introduce either Jay or the woman beside him.

"Andrea, this is Jay." That was it. No explanation of either relationship.

Jay stuck out his hand, "I'm Jay Clark. I'm Max's best friend. I've known him his whole life."

Andrea shook his hand, "I'm Andrea Dunlap, but my friends call me Bella. I'm Max's girlfriend."

Jay looked at Max but shook Bella's hand a little longer. "Girlfriend? How nice to finally meet you, *Bella*. How did you two meet?"

Bella laughed. "It's weird you should ask that. It's a funny story. We just started dating." She looked at Max who wasn't looking at either one of them, but had moved over a few steps and was leafing through a magazine on fishing. "We've been working for the same company for a couple of years, but I'd never even talked to Max until a few weeks ago. We both ended up in line next to each other for a marathon of Twilight movies! Max had never seen any of them, and just on a whim decided to see them. We met in the line and got to know each other. The rest is history."

Jay nodded, "Just on a whim? What a coincidence. When was that, Bella?"

Max grabbed him and pulled him down the aisle. I'll be right back, Bella. Jay wants to tell me something."

Jay was doubled over laughing by the time they reached the produce section, and Max let go of his arm. "Twilight? Really, man? How could you sink so low?"

Max looked around to make sure Bella couldn't hear him. "Are you kidding? Did you see her?"

Jay squinted and looked up at the ceiling. "Let me guess, was that Thursday the 20th by any chance? The day you borrowed that money from me?"

Max held up his hands, "Okay, okay, I'll tell you the whole story. I overheard her say at work that she loved these movies and was going to the marathon. I couldn't tell how much money was left on my debit card, so I borrowed the money from you for the movie. I got there early and waited in my car until she arrived. Then I ran over and got in line right behind her. We stood in a long line talking until the movie started. Then I sat near her. We hit it off, like I knew we would. Unfortunately, I slept through most of the movie. Then, I took her out to coffee with the ten I bummed."

Jay shook his head, "Uh, I think that you meant 'fortunately, you slept through the movie...'" He laughed. "Twilight! And you were

eavesdropping, too and stalking just like I did."
Then he realized the real reason Max hadn't
wanted to tell him the name of the church he was
going to visit. "Wait, I'll bet she's the one who
invited you to the church you 'forgot' the name of!
And you were going to 'save me from myself'!"

Max nodded. "Yeah. It was New Life. Go
ahead and stalk the Mad Coffee Lady if you want
to." He turned. "I have to go."

"She called me, and I've been over to her place
twice. She's making breakfast for me right now. I'm
here to pick up a couple of items for it." Jay
couldn't help feeling a little smug.

Max stopped and looked at Jay. "Isn't she a
little dangerous for you? I mean you're so picky
about your clothes, your condo, your car..."

"I'm hoping the crazy spills and head injuries
will end eventually."

"Head injuries? I'm sure there's a story behind
that, but you'll have to tell me later. I can't keep
Bel- I mean Andrea waiting."

"Yes, Maxim, don't keep *Bella* waiting." Jay
laughed and shook his head as Max hurried off.

Seventeen

By the time Jay arrived with the caramel rolls, Mad had changed into a pair of blue jeans and a pink long-sleeved T-shirt the same color as her bathtub. Jay thought it was a weird comparison, but he couldn't help making it. Frank accompanied him to the kitchen sniffing hopefully at the bag of food. Jay petted him and set the bag on the counter.

"Smells great in here," he said.

"I'll pop the rolls in the oven," Mad said.

She had set the small dining room table, but she was still cooking the food when he arrived. Jay stood in the corner of the kitchen, leaning on the counter. He hadn't watched anyone cook since he'd last visited his mother. He wondered if Mad knew how much he appreciated a home-cooked meal. He hoped he wasn't making her nervous. He didn't think he could take any more messes right now.

Mad had him sit down at the small dining room table and joined him with two brightly colored plates. She didn't seem surprised this time when he took her hands in his to bless the food. Jay looked at his plate. There were two slices of fried bread with eggs in the middle and more fried bread on the plate.

"Thank you, Father, for this food… whatever it is. Amen."

"It's Egyptian one-eyes," Mad took a bite and smiled while she chewed.

"You did use your imagination, didn't you?"

"It isn't squid. I believe that was your one

criterion."

"Egyptian Eyes," Jay was having a hard time getting past the name. "It sounds like a song."

"Egyptian one-eyes," she sang.

"I see two looking at me right now."

"You've never had this before, even as a kid? Some people call it Eggs in a Nest. You butter both sides of the bread, cut out a hole in the center of the bread, cook one side, turn it over, break an egg into the opening, then when it has set a little, you turn it over and cook the other side. And you cook the holes the same way. Use them to sop up the yolk. It's good. Try it." She continued eating.

Jay was willing to try the food; after all, he'd agreed to anything. He took a bite. It was good, much better than a regular fried egg with toast. "Delicious! So who taught you to make gourmet hot chocolate and exotic foods, your mom or your dad?" He ate both eggs, the center of the bread, and several rolls.

Mad took another caramel roll. "My dad and stoves are not simpatico."

Jay nodded. "I have one of those non-simpatico stoves, too."

"You don't cook?"

"Does cold cereal count?"

Mad smiled. "No."

"Sandwiches?

"Almost."

"I get a lot of takeout."

"Nowadays a lot of guys can fend for themselves in the kitchen."

I can fend for myself. I just can't cook. The

important thing is to be able to work your three basic kitchen appliances: the microwave, the can opener, and the refrigerator."

Mad laughed. "You've mastered the refrigerator, then? I've heard that's the hardest one."

"I was going to write a book on what I've learned. Always keep the food covered, and if you don't remember how old the food is, offer it to the dog first."

"No! You'd make your dog sick to save your skin?"

"You didn't let me finish. Riley has a very discerning nose. If he won't eat something, I chuck it."

"And if he will, isn't it too late?" Mad laughed.

"Yes, well there is that little problem, wrestling the food back from him."

Jay picked up his dishes to clear the table. Maddie started pushing him into the living room. "You go sit and relax. You worked on my gutters and saved my dog's life. You've done enough today."

"Mad, I cleared about four feet of gutter."

"Well, you saved Frank's life." She started filling the sink with soapy water.

"That's true; I am a hero." Jay sat down on the sofa. "I appreciate the meal you cooked for me. It was delicious."

"I'm glad you liked it. I was a little worried that you might be a health nut or something and wouldn't eat butter or eggs."

"I told you my favorite breakfast was caramel

pecan rolls, and you thought I might be a health nut?"

"I know it doesn't make sense. It's just that you look so fit and strong like you work out a lot..." Mad trailed off.

Maddie was so embarrassed! Why did she say that aloud? She returned to drying dishes. "I was just hoping you liked it," she finished hurriedly.

Jay came back into the kitchen. "So you think I look pretty strong, huh?" He flexed a bicep for her.

"Well, you know, um, sure." Maddie kept working on the dishes and didn't look at Jay.

"I'd love to stand around here talking about how good you think I look, but I have a column to write." Jay smiled and headed for the door with Maddie following. He stopped suddenly and turned around. Maddie ran into him. He laughed.

"Bye, Mad."

Jay walked through the door into the sunshine. He took a deep breath and jogged off in what she assumed was the direction of his apartment. Maddie let the door shut and leaned on it. Franky came over, tipped his head, and looked at her inquisitively. She stooped down and picked him up, nuzzling her cheek against his comforting, furry neck. "He's not so bad, is he Franky? You like him, don't you, boy?" Franky set to work, rapidly licking her face. Maddie lowered him to the floor, went to wash her face again, and reapply her makeup. This dog had caused more trouble in the last few weeks than the whole time she'd had him. He followed her into the bathroom and watched her. "It looks like yours are the only kisses I'll be getting for a while," she said. She tried to ignore the pang of disappointment admitting that to herself had caused.

Tiffany was laying low. McKenzie had no problem putting her up in her dorm when told about the apartment break-in. McKenzie was convinced it was someone stalking her. Someone following her might have been a closer description, but McKenzie reveled in the drama of being stalked. Tiffany found that odd. She'd been stalked in college and it was frightening. Tiffany had stressed the need for confidentiality. So far, McKenzie was keeping her promise, but it was taking its toll on her to keep her mouth shut.

The cat was another matter. Sneaking Ebony into the dorm and keeping her under wraps wasn't easy, but there was no way either she or the cat was going back to that apartment.

Tiffany canceled her date with Mitch, begging off on account of feeling out of sorts since the break-in. She needed some time to recuperate from the ordeal of that and her lost cat.

She considered letting Dalton know that her apartment had been broken into, but she didn't want to spook him. Maybe break-in wasn't connected to the information she'd sold him.

To be on the safe side, she called in sick every day, simply skipping work. She hung out at Georgetown, often with McKenzie, dressing in jeans and a T-shirt to fit in on the campus.

While Tiffany told her sister a little about the

break-in, she didn't tell Kate that she was staying at Georgetown, unwilling to put her sister, who was attending the same university, in danger. She almost ran into Kate one day, but her sister didn't notice her in the crowd standing with McKenzie in line for coffee. Tiffany wasn't surprised. Looking down at the borrowed clothes, Tiffany barely recognized herself. Her silky hair pulled into a ponytail completed the disguise. Tiffany never looked like this, even on her days off, and she abhorred the slightly messy, understated style (or lack of it). She wasn't herself. She'd never realized how much she relied upon her wardrobe. She grimaced. Tiffany hadn't spent years at university and building a career to look like a college kid.

Dalton's phone rang. He looked at the number and didn't bother with any niceties. "Yeah?"

"Clark just left again," said the unnamed caller.

Dalton gripped the phone harder. "So he was there once last night, and twice today?"

"Yeah."

"Keep tailing her," Dalton hung up.

So she had lied. Madison did leak that information on purpose to Clark. Time to set the trap. And she would deserve what happened when it snapped.

A few hours later, the senator called asking Maddie to come to his office to go over the speech he'd asked her to prepare. She barely had time to change since he told her he needed her at his office right away. She grabbed her laptop, thankful she'd finished the speech ahead of time. As she was getting into her car, Lizette called.

"Hi sis, I'm about to drive, so talk fast if you want to save my life."

"You mock, Maddie, but more people die in car accidents than…"

"Your nagging is cutting into my drive time. My boss just called asking for a speech that two days ago he gave me a week to write. Good thing I had it done."

"Unethical and flaky too," Lizette observed.

"I'm confused why it's suddenly so urgent. He doesn't need it until Wednesday. Why does he want it now?"

"I heard you start your engine," her sister accused.

"Am I trying to hide it from you?" Maddie asked.

"I don't want to be on the phone with you when you get into an accident. Did you call Dad?"

"Oh no, there's an 18-wheeler coming straight at me!"

"Bye," Lizette said flatly.

Maddie laughed and tossed her phone in her purse.

"Why *does* he want this speech now?" She wondered aloud.

Maddie looked in her rearview mirror. "Why would anyone want a black car in this climate? They're so hot in the summer. The real question is why am I talking to myself so much, now? I don't even have the dog around to blame it on. And now

165

traffic is going to make me late."

Maddie sighed in frustration as traffic slowed and halted. She pulled out her cell phone to check her messages. As she did, she started to chuckle. She had an idea.

Maddie grinned mischievously as she sent a text to Jay: "Going to senator's office 4 evidence." She immediately typed "jk" in a new message to let him know she was kidding and hit send. Traffic had started while she was playing with her phone, and a driver a couple of cars back laid on his horn. She quickly shut her phone and dropped it in her purse. She didn't notice when she closed it so quickly, the second message didn't send.

Dalton replaced the receiver on the phone and looked at the greasy man sitting across from him playing with his letter opener. "Are you sure you can do this?"

"Just leave it to me. It's my specialty." The small, dark-haired man tossed the letter opener on the desk and cracked his knuckles. He stood up. Dalton winced at the sound. It always brought up a vision of a skeleton's bones breaking.

"Where do you want me to be when she arrives?" The man asked, looking around the room while he waited for the senator's reply.

Dalton nodded toward the closet. "It will take a while for her to get here, though."

His visitor walked over to the couch, stretched himself out on it, and closed his eyes, clearly intending to nap. Dalton almost said something about the audacity of the man. Whose office was it anyway? And where did the DNC find him? What did they do, keep him on retainer? Dalton shrugged. As long as he didn't have to get his hands dirty, why ask questions?

Eighteen

Jay was just leaving his boss's office after getting his new assignment when his phone notified him he had received a message. He was excited when he saw it was from Maddie. As soon as he read it, though, he groaned and rubbed his forehead in exasperation. "'Going to Senator's office...' She promised not to do that!" he muttered to himself. He wondered for a second if she was kidding. Would she really do it? After he stressed to her that it was so dangerous? Why would she text him? Was she just teasing him? Was she like that? He knew so little about her. Maybe this was her twisted sense of humor. He couldn't take a chance. He pulled his keys out of his pocket and headed for his car. If she was foolish enough to sneak into the lion's den, she needed someone to set her straight.

Maddie arrived at Senator Stanfield's office and took the first available parking spot. She grabbed her purse and laptop and hurried as fast as her kitten heels would take her, still wondering why she was being hurried. The senator hadn't given her any details. Maybe he was leaving town unexpectedly. *I suppose he could have a family emergency. Although he's never mentioned having family, he must have one.*

In the outer office, Jeanie was gathering up her purse, preparing to leave. She buzzed the senator to announce Maddie's arrival, told her she could go in and left the office.

When Maddie entered the senator's plush office, he was sitting behind his desk, straightening some papers. He greeted her as he rose and moved to the table where they usually worked. She couldn't gauge his mood from the short greeting she received. He was being unusually quiet. When he sat down and opened his laptop, it was obvious he was checking his email. Maddie paused, eying the senator and wondering if it might be possible to sneak a look at his account. She laid her laptop on the table and mentally gave herself a lecture. She wasn't Maddie McPherson, Private Eye, maneuvering an angle to investigate her boss. She was simply a speechwriter; she was there to work.

She sat down next to him and had barely opened her laptop when the senator grunted in surprise and turned to her.

"Maddie, could you do me a favor? Senator Lee's courier left for the day without dropping off a copy of a bill I need to look at tonight. Could you run over and pick it up for me?"

Maddie was a little taken aback. Errand girl? Was that what she was called across town for? She searched for a way to graciously decline. She couldn't come up with anything, and the senator stared at her almost as if he were daring her to refuse.

Maddie shrugged. "Sure. What about your speech, though? Don't we need to go over it?"

The senator nodded toward her laptop, "Just bring up a copy of it, and I'll look through it while you're gone."

Maddie was alarmed. She wasn't normally a suspicious person, but with the information she'd gleaned from Senator Stanfield lately, she knew better than to trust her computer to him.

"Unless you don't trust me," he said quietly.

Maddie knew better than to take the bait for that trap. She quickly pulled a copy up and emailed it to him. "I'll just send you a copy. IT warned me when I started that I shouldn't allow anyone to use my laptop." She shut it down, put it in her satchel, and grabbed her purse. She considered taking it with her, but she knew running around in heels was going to be hard enough without lugging her computer.

"Which building is Senator Lee in?" She asked with her hand on the doorknob.

"He's in Russell."

Maddie was glad her boss was concentrating on bringing up a copy of the speech so he didn't see the look of dismay on her face. It would take half an hour at least for her to get over there and back! She'd already agreed to go, so she couldn't very well refuse now.

Maddie didn't say anything, knowing her voice would betray her. As she walked, though, she fumed. By the time she arrived at Senator Lee's office, her feet were already aching, and she still had to walk back.

"She's gone," Dalton Stanfield opened the closet door and led the way to a table with a laptop on it.

The small, dark man sat down in front of the

computer and said, "I thought you needed me to hack this. She's already logged on."

The senator closed his eyes, already starting to doubt the man's ability, convinced he was surrounded by absolute fools.

"That's my computer. Hers is in this bag." Dalton pulled out the laptop and placed it in front of the hacker who immediately turned it on and went to work.

"Okay, I need all the personal information you can give me, birth date, anniversary date, husband's or boyfriend's names, names of other family members, pets' names, all of her addresses. Anything she might use in her password," the hacker's hands hovered expectantly over the keyboard.

"I don't have any of that information." Dalton was exasperated. No one had told him he'd need to know all of that. "Can't you just use some computer software to get in? Are you just going to try to guess her password?"

"Yeah, we guess. That's how we get in. We don't have time for the software." The man leaned back and pulled a pack of cigarettes from his shirt pocket.

"There's no smoking allowed in this building." Dalton watched the man pause as though deciding if he were going to obey the rule. "Smoke gives me a migraine, too," Dalton added. Slowly the man put the cigarettes away.

"We've got only about a half-hour. Don't you have some generic passwords you could try?" Dalton knew since it was after hours, he wouldn't be able to access Madison's personnel file.

The man typed in a word.

"What was that?" Dalton nervously looked at his watch. How long had she been gone?

"Password. Some people use the word as their password." The little man grinned revealing teeth that hadn't seen a dentist in a long time. Dalton looked away trying to hide his disgust. "Some people got no imagination," the hacker said.

"Yes." Dalton agreed absentmindedly. He suddenly remembered Madison had a pet. "Wait, she has a dog. I heard her talking about him to my receptionist. She named the dog something that had to do with the breed. It was a dachshund. She named it hot dog or sausage or something like that. I remember Jeanie didn't get the joke at first."

The greasy man tried both ideas. "Nope."

Dalton thought some more, "Oscar Meyer, maybe?"

"Nope, that's not it either. Maybe combined with her birth date or one of her past addresses..."

"I told you, I don't have that information! And you'll have to do it today!" Dalton was exasperated. He knew he probably wouldn't be able to separate her from her laptop this easily again. She'd start to catch on.

"What was that mutt's name?" Dalton asked himself. He could feel his frustration growing. The hacker picked up a letter opener and started cleaning his nails with it. "Give me that!" Dalton grabbed it out of his hand cutting the man in the process.

The hacker gave him a menacing look and held

his thumb up to his mouth to catch the blood.

"I-I'm sorry. I didn't mean to," Dalton stammered out.

"Frankly I don't care if you didn't mean to…"

Suddenly it came to Dalton. "Franky! The dog's name was Franky!"

The man's fingers started to type and then stopped. "How do you spell that?"

"I don't know! Try F-R-A-N-K-I-E. If that isn't it, try a "y" at the end."

The man tried them both. "Nope. Neither one works."

Dalton remembered seeing Madison mouth the letters as she put in her password. It suddenly hit him why she had done that. "Try both those spellings backward," he suggested.

The man typed, hit enter, and a picture of a dog came up on the screen as the background. "We're in!"

"No thanks to you," Dalton wanted to say, but he restrained himself and passed the man a piece of paper. "Here's what I want you to do."

Nineteen

Jay arrived at the Hart Senate Building and found Senator Stanfield's office with no trouble since he had interviewed the Senator when Jay had first started at the paper. This was before Jay had marked Stanfield as one of several Congressional representatives whose duplicity needed watching and reporting. After the first article came out that Jay wrote about the senator and his questionable programs, Jay wasn't granted any more interviews.

There was no one in the outer office. Since Congress wasn't in session, the senator's staff must be on vacation. Jay wasn't sure what to do. Maybe he was about to get Mad in bigger trouble. He decided to see if the door was locked. Just as he reached for the knob, the door opened and a small, greasy man passed Jay and moved quickly through the outer office. Jay barely caught a glimpse of him. The senator didn't seem very surprised to see Jay, which surprised Jay.

"May I help you?" The senator stood in the doorway and Jay could tell he wasn't going to be invited in. He'd better avoid mentioning he was looking for Madison.

Jay pulled out the small, yellow pad of paper he carried to take notes on and clicked his pen. "I'm in the building on another errand, but while I'm here, I'd like your impressions on the latest developments in the Middle East." Jay tried to peek into the senator's office, but he couldn't see anyone. "I'm available for an extended interview if you're not busy."

The senator stood in the doorway, clearly not fooled. "I didn't schedule an interview with you."

Jay didn't budge. "I know we didn't have one scheduled, but since I'm already here, why don't you answer a few questions about the situation over there. It's a very popular topic in the news right now." Jay figured any politician wouldn't turn down free publicity.

"I won't be granting any interviews to you, Clark, and you know why." The senator made a motion to close the door.

Jay stuck his foot in the door. "Where's Madison?"

"Why do you want to know?" The senator's voice was flat, betraying no emotion.

Jay struggled to maintain his composure. What reason could he give?

The senator opened the door far enough to allow Jay to view the whole office. "As you can see, she's not here. You will either leave now, or I'm calling security."

Jay wanted to search the office. What if she were tied up in the closet? "Maybe I'll be the one to call security to make sure no harm has come to Mad."

"Why should any harm come to her here? What are accusing me of? Anyway, to whom do you think security would listen? A respected member of the Senate, or a pesky reporter?"

Jay clenched his teeth. "I don't know. Let's call them and find out," he dared.

"Look, Clark, I don't know what the

relationship is between you and my speechwriter, but any relationship between you two I see as a conflict of interest. Are you trying to get her fired?" The senator leveled a gaze at him that revealed nothing.

Jay stood his ground. "I wouldn't think a member of the unbiased, free press should be considered off-limits as a contact for any senatorial staff. Anyway, I barely know your speechwriter."

Stanfield crossed his arms across his chest. "I doubt that. If you 'barely know' her, why are you here riding in like the cavalry to save her? Although from what, I have no idea. And if you're unbiased, I'd hate to see what bias looks like."

"Oh, I think we could find an example of bias pretty easily from the liberal media who are tucked neatly in your pocket and won't say a word against you."

"If other media outlets support my causes and believe in my political career, who am I to dissuade them?"

"And I believe you just proved my point. They don't exist to get government officials elected and keep them in office. Their job is to report the news!"

The senator had obviously grown tired of the argument. "Are you leaving?"

Jay turned. "Yes, but if she doesn't show up soon, I'll be back."

"I'll have security on speed dial." The senator shut the door with a little too much force.

Maddie was almost back from her trek to the

senator's office. All she had been able to think about on the return trip from the Russell building were her sore feet. She halted when she saw Jay come out of the senator's office suite and was about to ask, "Why are you here?" One look at his grim face made words unnecessary as a horrible realization came over her that he had taken her joking text seriously.

When he caught sight of her, though, relief was the only emotion on his face. He grabbed her in a clumsy bear hug. Jay must have remembered where he was immediately because he released her. Maddie sank onto the bench outside of Senator Stanfield's office and kicked off her shoes.

Exhausted, but knowing she owed Jay an explanation, she pulled her phone out of her purse and checked her outgoing texts. Her "jk" wasn't among them. Jay sat next to her.

"I'm so sorry. I was kidding when I sent that text to you. I thought I immediately sent you another text saying it was a joke, but it must have been erased before it was sent."

Jay nodded. He looked like he was thinking something over. She knew they couldn't say any more so close to her boss's office. "I should have figured it was something like that. What a twisted sense of humor you have!"

Maddie slipped on her shoes and stood up. "I need to finish going over a speech with Senator Stanfield." The door to his office opened as if he had been standing on the other side waiting for her to say his name and the senator stepped through. He was carrying her satchel and his briefcase.

"Ah, Ms. McPherson back, safe and sound. Clark, it looks like you owe me an apology."

"Like that would happen."

The senator handed Maddie her satchel, set his briefcase on the bench, took the envelope she handed him, and put it in his briefcase. "The speech is fine, Ms. McPherson. I'll be in touch." And he walked away without another word.

Maddie stood glaring after her boss. The man could use a lesson in manners. "Not even a 'thank you' after I hiked over to Russell to pick up a copy of a bill that Senator Lee's courier forgot to drop off before he went home," she whispered fiercely to Jay.

Jay stared at her. "He used you as a courier?" He didn't attempt to whisper.

"Yes! As soon as I arrived, he sent me over to Russell to pick up that envelope. Then he didn't even say 'thank you'! My feet are killing me, and I still have to walk to my car." Jay put a hand on her arm.

"Mad, I would say that was not only rude; it was suspicious. Couriers work all hours of the day and night. They don't all punch out and go home at 5:00."

"He said he needed a copy of a bill."

"Congress isn't even in session!"

"Why would he have me run over there if he could get a courier to do it, especially since he didn't even need it! And I did it in heels!" Maddie took off her shoes.

"Maybe it had something to do with that little man who darted out of the office when I arrived."

Jay looked back at the door to Senator Stanfield's outer office.

"What little man?" Maddie kept walking.

"A greasy little man was leaving when I got here."

"I didn't see any man. Dalton was the only one there when I arrived."

"Dalton?"

"Senator Stanfield."

"I've never heard you call him 'Dalton' before," Jay explained.

"I used to call him by his first name. I usually don't anymore. I call him 'Senator.'"

"At one point, I thought you were interested in him," Jay said softly.

Maddie turned to him. "That was when I thought he had integrity. I know better now. Maybe we should look around." Maddie hesitated; then went over and tried the doorknob.

"What are you doing?" Jay asked.

"I, um, forgot something in here."

"Mad, security cameras don't have sound. You don't need to lie."

"I'm not lying. I forgot that piece of paper incriminating the senator." Maddie entered the outer office and tried the senator's door. It was locked.

"Can you pick this?" Maddie looked at Jay intently.

"Of course not!"

"I thought journalists know how to pick locks," said Maddie examining the doorknob.

"You watch too many movies."

"That may be true." Maddie poked around in her purse and pulled out a credit card.

"Seriously? Did you minor in breaking and entering?"

Shielding what she was doing from the security camera with her body, Maddie tried to no avail to pick the lock. She pulled out her keys.

"You have a key to his office?"

"I read somewhere that some keys are a close enough duplicate that they work."

"Close enough to a U.S. senator's office? Right. And where did you read that? Burglars Monthly?"

"They don't work. Here, give me yours." Maddie held out her hand expectantly.

"I am not going to be an accomplice to breaking into this office." Jay folded his arms across his chest.

"Maybe Jeanie has a key." Maddie moved toward the desk.

"A senator's secretary would not have an unlocked desk."

Maddie opened a drawer and started rifling through it.

"A senator's secretary would not leave a key to her boss's office lying around."

Maddie found a key and opened the door.

"There are some serious security breaches around here," Jay observed.

"We're in," Maddie whispered.

"You're in! I'm out!" Jay took a step toward the door nonetheless.

"Okay, you keep a lookout," Maddie whispered as she entered the senator's office and started going through his drawers.

"Another unlocked desk. Five to ten."

"What?" Maddie pulled out a file folder, leafed through it, and put it back where she found it. She dumped the contents of the wastebasket on the floor and started pawing through it.

"That's what you're going to get for this. Five to ten years."

Maddie wordlessly handed a piece of paper to Jay. He read it and turned it over, looking at the back.

"It was in the wastebasket. I wonder who told him to abstain from the vote. I'm taking it just in case it's useful later."

"That's theft."

"For stealing garbage? I might as well get something for my five to ten. Let's go."

Maddie put the garbage back in the wastebasket, and they hurried outside. Maddie looked around trying to remember where she'd parked. "I don't see my car. By the way, how did the senator react when you showed up?"

Jay looked a little sheepish. "He said I was 'riding in like the cavalry' to save you."

Maddie raised her eyebrows. "Really? Why did he say that?"

Jay looked around. "So where do you think you left your car? We should find it before it gets dark."

Maddie let him off the hook. She gestured to the corner of the lot. "I thought I parked it right here."

Jay walked behind a large van. "Here it is.

Hey, one good thing came out of today."

Maddie pulled out her keys, unlocked her car, and opened the door. "I get a prison record?"

Jay grinned. "There's no reason to avoid being seen together anymore. Before you're indicted, would you like to go out to dinner?"

"I still have a job, right?"

Jay shrugged. "As far as I know. In the meantime, let's find a quiet place to eat supper and you can tell me all about yourself. Where would you like to eat?"

"I haven't lived in D.C. long enough to know too many places outside my neighborhood. Anyway, since you're an investigative reporter, shouldn't you already know all of the interesting things about me?"

"You're right. I know you like dachshunds and Egyptian Eyes. What else do I need to know?"

"Egyptian one-eyes and there isn't much else."

"Yes, and I know how you like your coffee..."

Maddie punched Jay playfully, "We are not going there."

Jay raised his hands in defeat. "I give up. You win."

Maddie laughed. "You bet I do. And since you admitted defeat, I'll let you pick the restaurant."

"Okay, I haven't been to the Dupont Italian Kitchen lately."

"And I haven't been to it ever, so should I follow you?"

Jay held out his arm. "I'd rather you rode with me."

Maddie nodded and locked her car door.

"Let's go!"

Jay held the car door open for Maddie and bowed. "Ah ha! A gentleman," she said.

Neither of them noticed the small dark car that pulled out of the parking lot behind them and followed   at   a   distance.

Twenty

Jay knew he'd chosen well when they were seated on the patio of "The Kitchen" as locals called it. Jay had always enjoyed the food, but the interior was dark, and he usually sat outside if the weather was right. It was the perfect night to bring Mad. It was still warm, but not oppressively so. She looked around, kicked off her shoes, took a sip of water, and seemed to relax visibly. "Do you like Italian food?" he asked.

Mad laughed. "It's a little late, now, to ask me, isn't it?"

Jay thought it might be too soon to say he was already hoping they'd go out again, so he just laughed and agreed. He ordered Chicken Francaise and she ordered the seafood pasta.

He thought back to the times he'd first seen her at the Daily Grind and had thought about getting to know her. She hadn't seemed awkward or ditzy. There had been no spills or secrets revealed. She had seemed like a nice, normal girl with a regular, normal life. Sitting here, Jay suddenly felt that his first opinion had been restored. The last few weeks must have been an anomaly.

Jay later thought it was interesting that at the exact moment he had that thought, a waiter walked past their table, stepped on Mad's shoes, tripped, and dumped a generous helping of Caesar salad in a man's lap at a nearby table. The man grumbled, the waiter apologized, and Mad apologized profusely. Jay simply retrieved Mad's shoes and handed them to her. She put them back on her feet. There was no anomaly. Accidents followed her. Jay smiled and nodded weighing that thought. It was all right. He could live with that.

Mad searched the crowded area. "Where is our waiter? Let's get our food to go."

Jay had no intention of leaving. If spending time with Mad was going to be a series of this kind of thing, they couldn't keep leaving restaurants in the middle of a meal. They needed to finish dinner.

"Really? Do you want to leave? I'd think you'd be used to this by now."

"Used to what?"

"Spills, accidents, pratfalls."

"I am not a klutz!"

"Maybe you're just distracted. These things happen."

"They have been happening to me with alarming frequency."

"They happen to everyone."

Mad looked at him. "When did you last kick off your pumps because your feet hurt? And did the waiter grind your kitten heel into the pavement?" Mad took off her shoe and examined the heel, holding it up to the dimming light. "I loved these shoes!"

Jay looked at Mad sitting there looking so sad. "Are you in mourning? Can't you just buy another pair of red shoes?"

"Do you know how hard it is to find a perfect pair of shoes like this?"

"I thought they made your feet hurt."

"They aren't meant for walking."

"Why do women wear shoes that hurt their feet?"

"Because they're pretty."

"That's why I bought my last pair, too. Aren't they pretty?"

Jay stuck his feet out, almost tripping their waiter, who asked if they needed anything else, then left quickly.

"It's not contagious!" Maddie called after the waiter.

Jay ignored the waiter's behavior and took Mad's hands in his for prayer. "Father, thank You for this food, and thank You for this opportunity to get to know Mad. Amen."

"And save us from catastrophes involving shoes. Amen."

"Amen!" Jay echoed vehemently.

Jay took a bite of his chicken. Mad poked at her pasta, which was in a large bowl. He could see she was still upset over the salad spill.

"Seafood pasta... any squid in there?" Jay waited for Mad's reaction.

She laughed and twirled some pasta on her fork. "Yes, and I have no problem with squid. Except after eating it, I can't make a fist," she joked referring to an old Neil Simon movie she loved.

"Why can't you make a fist? Are you allergic to it?" Jay looked puzzled.

"Never mind. I was kidding," she said. "You wouldn't have ordered this, would you?"

"Never. I also am not interested in octopus, eels, or fish eggs in case you'd like to order any of those the next time we go out." Jay avoided looking at Mad. He'd forgotten he was going to let her see how this date went instead of just assuming she'd want to go on another date with him. He already knew that he wanted to see her again. Mad didn't seem to notice what he'd said.

"So if I offer you a bite, you won't take me up on it?"

Jay looked over her bowl. "I like fish, shrimp, and scallops, but if I eat your seafood, all you'll be left with are the noodles."

Mad lifted another bite to her mouth. "And the squid."

"And the squid," Jay agreed. Despite the tripping incident, he felt very comfortable sitting here with Mad. It was so pleasant, he hated to bring up the senator again, but he had to. "I wonder what Stanfield was up to when he sent you out of his office."

Mad was in the middle of a bite. She swallowed before answering. "Why did he have to be up to something? Couldn't he just have made a mistake?"

Jay wished it could be so. "Mad, Stanfield knows how things work in Washington. This isn't his freshman term. Couriers, not speechwriters, carry bills. He's up to something."

Mad looked serious. "What could he be doing?"

Jay shook his head. "I don't know, but I'll tell you this. If he doesn't want whatever it is to be known, it may not be. He isn't afraid of the press. He has so many news outlets in his vest pocket that will say whatever he tells them. It's getting increasingly hard to get the truth out. The press has been called the fourth branch of government with good reason. It has a lot of power."

Mad's appetite had obviously returned; she speared a piece of seafood. As she lifted it to her mouth, she looked as if something occurred to her. She froze and dropped her fork back in her bowl. "My laptop!"

Jay took another bite of his chicken. It was delicious. "Your laptop is in my car," he said.

Mad shook her head. "The senator wanted to use my laptop to read the speech I brought to go over with him."

Jay looked serious. "You didn't give him access to your computer, did you?"

Mad looked equally serious. "What do you mean by 'give him access'? I emailed the speech to him while I was in his office, rather than allow him to use my computer, but I did leave my laptop there while I went over to Russell."

Jay put his fork down. "How long were you gone?"

Mad shook her head. "I don't know - at least half an hour."

Jay considered this. "I wonder if the senator and that other man did something to your laptop while you were running that errand. We need to check your computer." Jay saw Mad was looking around for the waiter again. "Let's finish our meal first. Then we'll see if we can figure out what the senator wanted with your computer."

"I shouldn't have trusted him!" Maddie slammed her hand down on the table, hitting her fork, which catapulted through the air hitting their waiter. He turned around with a pained expression.

"Check please!" Jay said.

"Let's leave him a big tip," Maddie whispered. Jay nodded.

Maddie had wanted to leave at the beginning, as soon as the waiter stepped on her shoes and tossed that salad into her poor neighbor's lap. She stole a glance in the man's direction now, but he'd already left. She didn't blame him. Salad greens had been clinging to him, and the parmesan cheese had stuck where it had landed on his pants in globs of Caesar dressing.

She truly wasn't this clumsy. She never had been before anyway. Maybe something about Jay caused people around him to spill things.

She could tell from his writing that he felt passionate about the Washington political scene, yet he was a calm person. Was he enjoying himself as much as he seemed to be? He'd just casually mentioned going out with her again. Who would do that after the scene that had just taken place? Of course, Jay should be used to it by now. He was probably convinced all she did was cause accidents. Yet there he sat, acting as though nothing had happened.

Jay paid the bill in cash. She thought that was odd. Doesn't everyone use a debit or credit card now?

"Let's go." Jay stood up and led the way through the crowded patio.

As soon as Maddie reached Jay's car, she opened up her laptop and logged on. She looked at her desktop. It looked the same. "What am I looking for?" She asked Jay.

"I don't know. Does anything seem out of place or different? Cyberly, that is."

Maddie looked at Jay. "'Cyberly'? Is that a word?"

Jay laughed "Why not? If it isn't, it should be."

Maddie looked through her emails. Everything seemed normal. "I don't see anything."

"We're almost to your car. After I drop you off, let's head over to your apartment, and I'll look at your computer, too." Jay pulled into the parking lot by the Senate buildings where Maddie had left her car. Maddie got out, turned around, and leaned into the car to grab her laptop and purse. She felt off-balance emotionally with the uncertainty of the computer problem, but she smiled weakly at Jay. He reached out and put his hand on her arm. "It's going to be okay," he said.

Maddie thought how nice it was to have him there reassuring her. "Yeah. I'll see you at my place." She quickly got into her car.

It had grown dark, and the only other car in the lot near them was a small, black car with tinted windows. Jay waited until Mad was in her car and on her way before pulling out of the lot behind her.

He arrived at her apartment right after she did and followed her up the steps. Jay noticed Mad locked the door as soon as she entered, even before she kicked off her shoes and turned on the lights.

He wondered if she was a little skittish because of what had happened at the Hart building. Handing him the computer, she picked up her shoes and unceremoniously dropped them in a nearby metal wastebasket with a thud as she headed for the kitchen. He decided it was better not to mention her actions.

"Would you like something to drink?" she called from the kitchen.

Jay sat on the couch, set the laptop on the coffee table, and turned it on. "Sure."

Mad appeared in the doorway. "What would you like? I have the same choices as last time."

Jay didn't hesitate. "I'd like the gourmet hot chocolate."

Mad laughed and went back into the kitchen. "It isn't gourmet. It's just homemade."

"It's gourmet to me," Jay said. "I'm used to Swiss Miss. You'll need to put in your password before I can do anything," he said.

"It's Franky spelled backward," she called back.

Jay went to the kitchen doorway. "I know a computer nerd, and he says to guard your passwords with your life. You shouldn't give it out like that."

Mad turned around and smiled. "Why? Can't I trust you?"

Jay returned to the couch. "It just isn't a good idea to give them out to anyone. Keep them secret."

Mad brought in a plate of chocolate chip cookies and set them next to the computer. "Well, you aren't just anyone."

Jay looked up and smiled, but Mad had returned to the kitchen. He wasn't hungry, but he couldn't resist what were obviously homemade cookies. He grabbed one and took a bite as he logged on. "Mmmm, chewy. Very good cookies."

Mad came back carrying two mugs of hot chocolate, both topped with whipped cream. She set them both on the coffee table and sank into the couch next to him. "My secret is I melt the butter before I mix the ingredients. Oops, there I go again, revealing my secrets."

Jay thought back to the first time he'd visited Mad at her apartment. He had sat on this couch. Mad had sat on the chair, and he'd thought at the time that she sat there because she was trying to get away from him. Looking back, she probably was. She'd certainly dressed in a way to let him know she wasn't interested in him. Now she seemed so relaxed, maybe a little too relaxed. She looked tired.

He took a cautious sip as he studied her files. "I don't see anything odd, but I think you need to have someone look at this. I have a friend who's a computer expert."

"Do you think the senator gave me a virus?" Mad leaned back against the couch cushion and closed her eyes.

"No. Why would he? Do you have material on here that could be permanently deleted because it isn't saved anywhere else? Even if you did, he wouldn't know that." Jay took another cookie. "These are the best chocolate chip cookies I've ever had."

Mad opened her eyes and smiled. "Best hot

chocolate, best cookies... You are just full of compliments tonight."

Jay shook his head, "I didn't say it was 'the best hot chocolate I'd ever had.' I said it was 'gourmet hot chocolate.'"

Mad swatted him. "Oh you know it's the best you've ever had."

Jay smiled. "Yes, it is."

Mad logged off and closed her computer, looking concerned. "Well, I guess there's nothing I can do until tomorrow."

Jay drained his mug and stood up. "I'd better be going."

Mad stood up, too, and put a hand on his arm. "Oh, I wasn't trying to get you to leave."

"You look tired anyway," Jay said.

"Thanks for that," said Mad.

"But in a pretty way."

"Right."

Jay laughed. She did look pretty, but he could tell she was very tired. It was time to go and let her get some rest. As he walked to the door, he knew he had to help her figure out what the senator was trying to do.

"Put your purloined evidence in a safe place and call me tomorrow. I want to help." He squeezed her arm and left.

Maddie closed the door and collapsed on the couch. Franky jumped up next to her and lay his head in her lap. "What just happened, boy? I didn't mean to chase him off." Franky looked up at her sympathetically. "Is he helping me just because he feels like he caused this whole thing? Because he feels sorry for me?" It was a depressing thought.

Someone knocked on the door. Maddie stood up and dragged herself to it. She hadn't realized she was so tired. It was Jay.

She opened the door. "Hi, Jay. Did you forget something?"

Jay said, "Yes, I did. I forgot this." He stepped inside the house and kissed her. Franky started barking.

"He's jealous," said Jay.

"He's protective."

"He might as well get used to it." Jay kissed her again. Franky barked. When the kiss was over, Jay looked at Maddie. Her eyes were still closed. He said, "You are tired," and left.

Maddie was stunned. She stood there without moving for several seconds before closing and locking the door. While clearing the dishes from the coffee table, she asked again, "What just happened?" She sure hadn't seen that coming. She smiled. She had been starting to think Jay saw this as only a friendship between two random people thrown together because of circumstances.

She quickly washed the few dishes and put the uneaten cookies back in the lighthouse cookie jar. Franky followed her into the bathroom as she got ready for bed. After a few minutes, he crawled into bed and lay his head on the other pillow waiting for her to join him. Maddie was exhausted. She fell asleep so fast that she barely had time to consider the possibilities of the kiss.

Twenty-one

Jay had looked at Mad for a second before he turned and left. She didn't say anything. She just stood there. Was it because she was so tired? What was she thinking? He wasn't going to stick around and analyze their relationship. After all, it was just a kiss, wasn't it?

"...analyze their relationship"? Why was he using that term? Since when did they have a relationship?

He quickly went down the steps and headed toward his car. As he pulled out his keys, he noticed a small, black car parked in front of the house next door. Wasn't that the same car he'd seen when he'd dropped off Mad by the Hart building earlier in the evening?

Jay started toward the car at the curb. Before he'd taken many steps, the engine started, and the car disappeared down the street. Jay considered pursuing it, but after all, most little cars looked alike, and it wasn't illegal to park on the street. He shrugged and got in his car.

When he arrived home, he dropped his keys on the table by the door and took time to pet Riley for a long time. "I haven't been home much today, have I, buddy?" It was already getting late, but his dog needed exercise, so Jay changed into his running clothes and grabbed a leash. The dog followed him around in excitement. As Jay kneeled to snap on the dog's leash, Riley turned toward the door and started growling. Jay heard a light tapping. "Come in," he called.

The front door opened a crack and Jay could see Max peering through. "Max, Riley hasn't ever hurt you, and anyway, I've got him on a leash."

Max opened the door and stepped inside. "Are you just coming back from a run or going out?"

Jay petted Riley. "We're just going out. Do you want to come with us?"

"No, I just wanted to borrow your tennis racket. Bella and I are going to play, and she doesn't have one."

Jay dropped the leash and started toward the closet. Max picked up the leash and handed it to Jay.

"I'll get it," he said. Max walked to the coat closet door and pulled out a racket and a couple of tennis balls.

Jay petted Riley. "No racket, huh? Does she even know how to play?"

"No, she's never played before. This is my chance to shine." Max did a forehand and a backhand swing. "How are you and the speechwriter doing? Has she spilled any burning hot liquids on you lately?"

Jay laughed. "No. Some more things have happened, but it wasn't her fault. I'll have to call you tomorrow and explain it all. We might need your help with a computer problem, too."

"Sure. Spills, head injuries, and loss of limb happen all around her, but they have nothing to do with her - except she's an accident magnet. The Spirit of Murphy's Law has possessed her."

Jay shook his head. "No loss of limb so far."

"Knock on wood." Max started bouncing a ball on the racket.

"What's happening with Bella? Seen any more 'Twilight' movies?" Jay said.

Max swung the tennis racket a few more times. "So far, no 'Twilight.' Also, I am happy to say no people have been burned or maimed in the course of this relationship."

Jay looked thoughtful. "Relationship? Are you already calling it a relationship? You just met her."

Max nodded. "Well, she started calling me her boyfriend almost immediately."

Jay interjected, "Which is surprising considering it's you."

Max objected, "Hey, it's not like this is my first girlfriend."

Jay said, "That's true. There was Jillian Schmidt."

"She was not my girlfriend."

"Max, I saw you kiss her at least a dozen times."

"She kissed me! You know she used to follow me around or wait by my locker and used every opportunity to grab me and hug me or kiss me!"

"You know you liked it."

Max considered. "Well, looking back it wasn't as bad as I thought at the time, but still, it was high school, and she did embarrass me."

"I always thought it was pretty funny," Jay said.

"You would. You always were easily amused. You'd think she would have realized there might have been a chance for her if she hadn't thrown herself at me."

Jay laughed. "Whatever. You wouldn't have dated her. All you had time for in high school was sports. And computers," he added.

"Yeah, well did you date anyone except Hannah what's-her-name?"

"White. Remember you kept calling her Vanna White and saying she should practice turning over letters?"

"Oh yeah. I wonder what happened to her. You dated for only about what... a week?"

"It was almost a month, and I have no idea what happened to her."

Max started toward the door. "Well, I have to get going. Bella is waiting."

"Isn't this the same way our last conversation ended?"

"Probably. Bella doesn't like to be kept waiting."

"The only time you drop by anymore is to borrow something. Don't you want to shoot some hoops sometime?"

Max winced. "Yeah, well, Bella takes up a lot of my time. I don't know if I could get away long enough to do that at this point in our relationship."

Jay laughed. "What you mean is that Bella won't let you play basketball."

Max nodded sheepishly. "Kind of. I've got to go. Bye!" He took the steps two at a time and drove away quickly. Jay and Riley followed more slowly down the stairs.

They did their usual route heading toward the park. When they reached Mad's house, he noticed the black car was parked in front of her house this time. He jogged slowly toward it. The car started and took off again. Jay could barely see the driver because the windows were tinted, but he could make out enough of the driver's face to think he looked familiar. All of the lights at Mad's house were out. She must have been exhausted and gone to bed as soon as he left. Maybe that was why she hadn't really reacted to his kiss.

Jay started jogging again. He'd have to call her or text her in the morning to be on the lookout for that suspicious car with that familiar driver.

Twenty-two

Maddie woke to Franky licking her on the mouth. She pushed him off and wiped her face with the back of her hand. Franky laid down on her pillow and sighed.

"Sorry, boy. I did say I wanted to be kissed, didn't I? And then I was... by Jay!"

She started to get out of bed. "Wait, he did kiss me, right? I hope that wasn't a dream." She'd had dreams before that seemed so real she thought they'd happened. She tried to remember, but she'd been so tired and her feet were so sore, that all that came to her was Jay saying a line about forgetting something, the kiss, and he was gone. She was sure the recollection was real, but it was a little hazy.

Maybe she should call him. Maybe he would mention the kiss. Her phone rang from the bedside table where it was plugged in, charging. "This is eerie," she said.

But it was only Lizette calling. "Hello," Maddie said sounding disappointed.

"Well, 'hello' to you, too," Lizette's said. "Doesn't my name pop up on your phone? It's known as 'call screening.' You don't have to talk to me if you don't want to."

Maddie was instantly sorry for making her sister think she wasn't happy to hear from her. She hadn't talked to Lizette in days. "I want to talk to you. I just thought you were going to be someone else."

Lizette's voice came back with a teasing tone.

"Would that someone else happen to be a certain handsome journalist? How's it going with you two?"

Maddie tried to remember how much she'd told her sister about Jay. "I made him breakfast yesterday, and we went out to dinner last night."

"Oh, this sounds very encouraging. I can't remember the last guy you dated. What's Jay like?"

Maddie got out of bed and padded toward the kitchen to make her morning coffee. "Well, as you said, he's handsome, very fit. I thought he was a personal trainer when I first met him. He has very strong morals..."

"Now are you sure of that this time?" Her sister interjected. "I seem to recall you thought the same thing of that slimy senator you work for."

"Leave it to the big sister to get right to the heart of a matter and remind you of every mistake you've ever made. Yes, Lizette, I'm sure this time. You'll have to come to D.C. to visit me and meet him." Maddie measured coffee as she spoke. "Oh, also, I came across some information proving my boss is mixed up in some dirty politics."

"Are you going to quit?"

"You must think I'm independently wealthy, Liz."

"I thought you were ethical."

"I think I can do more on the inside."

"This isn't about having a paycheck?"

"Nothing wrong with getting paid. I do work, you know."

"Oh, believe me, I know. Has he kissed you yet?"

"Senator Stanfield? No."

"The journalist!" her sister exclaimed.

The kiss. "As a matter of fact, he did last night."

"I certainly hope he's a gentleman."

"Don't worry, sis, he's a Christian."

"Yeah, well, a lot of guys say they're a Christian, but they convert at the first opportunity."

"Convert?"

"Into an octopus!"

Maddie ignored that last comment. "It was kind of a sudden thing. He'd already left. Then he came back, and when I asked him if he'd forgotten something, he said, 'Yes, I forgot this,' and he kissed me. Then he left again." Maddie looked in the basket holding the grounds. She'd gotten all caught up in her story and hadn't noticed how much coffee she'd put in. She took out the filter and dumped the grounds back into the canister and started measuring again.

"He's a writer, and the best thing he can come up with is, 'I forgot this'? How lame is that!"

Maddie didn't appreciate her sister's summation of her and Jay's first kiss, but before she could comment further her sister said, "What in the world?"

"What?" Maddie said as she hit the start button on her brewer.

"You're on TV!"

"What!"

"You are on TV. You're on the news! Wait, let me turn up the sound."

Maddie ran into the living room and turned on her TV. Before she could ask her sister what station Lizette was watching, an announcer came on with Maddie's high school picture in the corner. She grabbed the remote from a couch cushion and turned up the sound just as a reporter came on interviewing her boss. He looked at the camera as he spoke rather than the reporter.

"It has come to our attention that Madison McPherson, my speechwriter, contacted a member of the Democrat party, offering to sell 'a high-ranking official's campaign secrets,'" the senator read the last part from a piece of paper.

"Is Ms. McPherson still employed as your speechwriter?"

"She's been terminated," the senator said flatly.

"What?" said Maddie loudly.

"And Senator Stanfield, how has this affected you?" The reporter pointed the microphone in the senator's direction.

"I am deeply shocked, appalled at her behavior. I had put my utmost trust in Ms. McPherson, giving her access to my files."

"So, when you said 'a high-ranking official,' do you mean you?"

The senator nodded gravely, "Well, I assume..."

"Will there be an investigation into Ms. McPherson's alleged indiscretion?"

The senator looked startled. "Well, I would call this more than simply an indiscretion. This is a crime."

The reporter nodded, "And will there be an investigation into Ms. McPherson's alleged crime?"

Senator Stanfield nodded. "Oh, most assuredly, yes."

"This is Jordan Jacobs coming to you from the steps of the Capitol. Jill, back to you."

The news anchor came on the screen. "Thank you, Jordan. Next up, why are some House Republicans proposing President Smith be impeached?"

Maddie turned off the TV. Stunned, she sat down on the couch and felt something underneath her leg. She'd sat on her phone. She must have dropped it without noticing. She picked it up from the couch but could hardly speak.

"Lizette, are you still there?" she choked out.

"Of course I'm still here! What has that snake done to you?"

"I don't know anything about anyone's campaign secrets."

"Of course you don't. You're honest, which is more than I can say for your boss."

"Ex-boss." Maddie rubbed her hand across her forehead.

"Ex-boss," said Lizette. "And good riddance to him. I wonder what he has up his sleeve. Typical politicians - they're sneaky and deceitful. They'll outright lie to get into office, then turn around and accuse normal, honest citizens of crimes."

"I don't have a job," Maddie sank onto the couch.

"Do you have any money saved up?" asked Lizette.

"Not much, I've been trying to pay off my student loans."

"You always have a place with us if you need it," Lizette offered quickly.

"Thanks, sis, but I'm only four months into a year lease." Maddie looked around her small apartment.

"Right will win out, Maddie; you'll see."

"I'd better go, Lizette. I want to see what Jay thinks about this."

"Okay. Let me know what happens. I'll be praying for you. Bye!"

"Bye." Maddie looked at the phone in her hand. Her sister had said she would be praying for her. Maddie needed to pray, too. Before she ran to Jay, whom she barely knew, with her troubles, she needed to ask her Heavenly Father who had always been with her in the past. Maddie put down the phone and got on her knees. "Dear God, I feel so helpless. What do I do? Please help me."

Dalton thanked the reporter and headed for his office. The interview had been filmed on the Capitol steps because Dalton wanted it to look like Jordan Jacobs just happened to catch him at work going into the Capitol building. In reality, he'd called Jacobs and arranged to meet him here. The reporter was more than happy to show up with a camera crew immediately. Since Congress wasn't in session, a good reporter would have asked why he should meet the senator there. Dalton had chosen it because the Capitol building was the perfect backdrop. Too bad Dalton hadn't been able to get a shot a little farther away so he could've included the whole building. That would have been an impressive shot.

His phone rang; he didn't recognize the number. Maybe his plan was already showing results.

"Dalton Stanfield," he said confidently.

"Senator, I just saw your interview. Is this your idea of a joke?" It was Tiffany.

"No, this is my idea of a trap," he said.

There was a pause. "And Madison is the bait?"

"Obviously."

"Seems like overkill to bait a trap with a dove."

"She's not as innocent as she seems," he said grimly.

What if the DNC doesn't catch on?"

"I'm sure they will," he said.

"It may take some time," said Tiffany.

"A day or two at most."

"I hope you know what you're doing," she said shortly and disconnected.

But was the interview enough to get the ball rolling on his plan? He was hoping someone from the DNC would see it and catch the reference to a high-ranking government official's campaign secrets and wonder if it referred to the presidential scheme they'd been cooking up. Maybe Darrell Washburn himself would contact him. "A day or two at most," he repeated. "A trap too quickly sprung sets the prey free."

Tiffany slowly put her phone in her purse. What was happening? This was supposed to be just a simple trade: her information for some green. Innocent people weren't supposed to lose their jobs. *Or their lives.* Was that the next step? She knew all along that was a definite possibility playing with the big boys in the party; that's why she was more comfortable making money off the information than using it herself in some way. Why did Stanfield drag Madison into his plan? She reminded her of Kate, so naïve. She shook her head. It was out of control.

Twenty-three

Jay dropped his spoon in his Cheerios splattering milk on his glass coffee table. The last thing he'd expected to see when he turned on the news this morning was Mad being accused of a crime. The senator certainly hadn't wasted any time smearing her name. Jay should have known the politician had already set Mad up. He'd been too glib when Jay tried to enter the senator's office. That man exiting just when Jay arrived must have been involved. Jay wished he'd gotten a better look at his face.

Jay grabbed a paper towel from the kitchen to wipe up the spilled milk, but by the time he returned, Riley was doing the job for him. As Jay took his bowl into the kitchen, he grabbed a bottle of window cleaner and wiped off the table. He wondered if Maddie had seen the news yet. Now she really was out of a job. Stanfield had announced it on TV. Jay picked up his cell to call her, but he dreaded telling her the bad news. She had seemed so relaxed and happy last night, joking around with him. Would she blame him? After all, it was his fault. Would any of this have happened if he hadn't met her? Wouldn't she have gone blithely on, writing speeches for the senator? Jay was sure she had been set up because of her association with him after she innocently leaked that information in the coffee shop.

Before Jay called Mad, he needed a plan. He hit Max's number. This wouldn't be the first time he'd needed Max's expertise with computers, but it would be the most important.

Maddie finished praying and went into the kitchen to pour herself a cup of coffee. She had no idea what she was going to do to clear her name, but she remembered while she was praying that Jesus had said in His Word, "Lo, I am with you always." She wasn't alone.

She returned to the living room, set her cup on the coffee table, and grabbed her great-grandmother's afghan even though she wasn't cold. It was comforting just covering up with it. Her ancestor must have had a much simpler life. She was sure her great-grandmother had never faced anything like this. "But she could have been falsely accused and had her reputation attacked. That could happen to anyone." Franky jumped up on the couch next to her and snuggled up putting his chin on her leg. She petted him. He was comforting, too.

The phone rang. It was Jay. "Hi, Jay."

"Hi, Mad. How long have you been up?"

"I've seen it." Maddie felt resigned rather than shocked as when she'd first heard.

"I'm sorry. If I hadn't written that article..."

Maddie shook her head. "No, Jay. We both know who's to blame, and it isn't you."

"Well, I've been talking to computer geek I know. He's going to look at your laptop during his lunch hour today. We'll see if he can figure out what happened."

Maddie felt a huge relief at having a next move

to make. "Thank you, Jay, I didn't know anyone to call."

"I'm glad to help in any way I can." She could hear him clear his throat. "Mad, if you need any money..."

Maddie took a sip of coffee. She hadn't known him very long. "I appreciate the offer, Jay, but I'm sure I'll be fine." Okay, that was a lie, but she said it anyway. She wasn't going to take money from a guy she'd just met.

"The offer still stands in case you need any in the future."

God was already sending help. She wasn't alone. Lizette, Jay, and his friend all were ready to help her.

"Can you be here by noon? My friend, Max, will be here a little after that."

"Sure, and I'll need your address. How about I bring lunch since Max is being so nice."

Jay gave her his address. It was only a couple of blocks away. "Are you going to be okay until then?"

Maddie smiled. "I'll be fine, Jay."

"Well, I have to get to work. I'll see you soon. Goodbye."

"Bye." Maddie put her phone on the table and sank onto the couch. She took another sip of coffee. At least there was a plan. She hoped Max would be able to figure out what had happened.

If she was going to fix lunch for a couple of hungry guys, she was going to have to go to the store. Even though it wasn't chili weather, she decided to make it anyway. She had a good cornbread recipe she'd make, too. She couldn't sit here feeling sorry for herself. She needed to get going. She drained her cup and stood up. "Franky, life goes on, even if your career is in shambles." Franky looked up at her. "Even if my career is in shambles, that is," she said. She shook herself. She needed to focus on what she could do and not give up hope.

When Jay pulled into his condo parking lot during his lunch hour, he saw Mad standing next to her car waiting for him. She had a pot with a cord next to her on the hood and a metal pan. Her satchel and purse were over her shoulder. As soon as Jay parked, he met her at her car.

"Hi," he said and gave her a quick kiss on the cheek, wondering if she would think he was being too forward. He wasn't sure, yet, how she felt about last night's kiss. Well, even Paul had told the early Christians to "Greet one another with a holy kiss." You couldn't get more holy than a kiss on the cheek. He'd received kisses that were more amorous than that from his grandmother.

Jay handed Mad his keys and picked up the pot. "I'll get this. You unlock the door."

"I can carry a pot, Jay," she said.

"Safer this way," he said and carried it to his condo. Through the glass lid, he could see it was some kind of red soup, maybe chili, and he wanted to make sure it ended up in his kitchen on the counter rather than in his living room on the rug. The cord was the deal-breaker. He was sure tripping was a sure thing if Mad carried it.

Riley met them at the door and sniffed Mad, but he seemed to take a bigger interest in the pot Jay was carrying. Mad stopped to lay her purse and satchel on the dining room table, but the dog accompanied Jay to the kitchen and sat next to the pot expectantly.

She caught up with them in the kitchen. Jay gestured from Mad to Riley. "Mad, meet Riley, Riley, Mad."

She laughed. "We've met before. Not quite so formally, but we've met."

Jay nodded. "Oh yeah, the bush." Riley was sniffing the pot. He was so tall, he could reach the counter. "No Riley, leave it alone. Get down." Riley lay down on the floor.

Mad laughed again. "He reminds me of Franky, always looking for a handout." She started to hold out her hand, then hesitated and drew it back. "Will he eat me if I pet him?"

Jay shook his head. "Nah, he's gentle."

Maddie stooped and petted Riley who laid his head in her lap. Jay nodded in satisfaction. "I knew he'd take to you." Just like his owner, he thought.

Maddie looked around the kitchen. "Nice place, very neat."

Jay looked around trying to see it as Mad did. Mad's apartment was neat, too, but in a homey, lived-in way. Max was right when he'd said it was kind of cold looking in here.

There was a knock on the front door, and Jay went to let Max in. When Jay had called to ask him if he would look at Mad's computer, Max had made a joke about the laptop being booby-trapped,

212

but he had readily agreed to help. Jay hoped he wouldn't mention Mad's clumsiness in front of her.

When Riley heard the knock on the door, he scrambled up, toenails digging unsuccessfully into the tile and tore through the house. When he reached the front door, he ran straight for Max who quickly dodged behind Jay.

Jay laughed and walked away from the door. "He can sense if you act afraid of him."

Max kept Jay between Riley and himself. "I am afraid of him."

Mad stood in the kitchen doorway smiling.

Jay commanded, "Down, Riley." Riley lay down and Max seemed to relax. "Madison McPherson, meet my best friend, Max Bennett."

Max came out from behind Jay, and Mad got a good look at him. She pointed, jabbing her finger in the air. "I know you!" Max looked sheepish. "I mean I've met you at church. You're dating that one girl... what's her name?" Mad paused as though mentally snapping her fingers.

"Bella," Max offered.

"Really? What a coincidence since she seemed obsessed with that vampire movie," Mad said.

Max said, "Her name is Andrea Dunlap, but she identifies with Bella from the Twilight series, so she's taken that as a sort of nickname."

"Charming," said Mad aloud, but she whispered to Jay, "Scary!"

Jay laughed, "Yeah, it's all fun and games until one dark night she slips during a kiss and ends up going for your throat!"

"Ha ha. Where's the computer you want me to

work on?" Max looked around.

Mad pulled her laptop out of her satchel, turned it on, and logged on. Jay stood next to the table. Max sat at the table and cracked his knuckles. Mad winced, but she didn't say anything.

"So what exactly happened?" Max twisted around in his chair looking at Jay and Mad.

"I left my computer with my boss while I ran an errand, and while I was gone he must have sent an email to someone, purportedly from me."

"Purportedly?"

Jay put his hands on Max's shoulders. "Focus, man."

Max turned back around. "Probably had a hacker. Do you have an easy-to-remember password?"

Mad nodded. "It's my dog's name spelled backward."

Max took a deep breath. "Rule number one: don't give out your password to people. Guard it with your life."

"I didn't. He must have guessed it."

"Did your boss know your dog's name?"

Mad shrugged. "He could have. I've probably mentioned him to the senator."

"Rule number two: don't have a password that someone could guess."

Jay interjected. "Hey Max, could we skip computer safety class and get down to what happened?"

"Sorry. I tend to get a little carried away. What kind of email account do you have, Madison?"

"G-mail."

"And I suppose you have it set to automatically log you in, right?"

Mad nodded.

"Bad idea, but it's too late to talk about that now. When did this happen?"

"Yesterday evening around 5:00."

Max looked hopeful. "Well, since it's Google, it could still be on their server." He typed for a while. "Whatever was sent has been deleted from your computer."

"What good will it do if Google has a record of it? Wouldn't it show it came from my computer? It won't show who was using my computer."

"It will show what time the email was sent. You couldn't be in two places at one time. You could find a witness," Max said.

Maddie perked up. "That's true!"

Jay said, "I suppose she'll need a subpoena to get whatever information Google has. You'll need an attorney, Mad."

Mad nodded. "Yeah, I guess I should have called one already. I was accused of a crime on national television by a U.S. senator."

Max whistled. "Yep, you need a lawyer. Uh, Jay, you mentioned lunch."

Mad took a deep breath. "I hope you like chili." They all started walking toward the kitchen.

Jay said, "Don't worry. If it's food, Max will eat it."

Dalton paced around his office. It had always seemed fairly spacious, but now it was boxing him in. He checked his email and his phone again. No email, no call. He collapsed on the couch.

His cell rang. He leaped for the phone, which he'd left on his desk. It was Tiffany.

"Did they bite?"

"Not even a nibble."

"You're going to have to be more forthcoming."

"If I do, there's no going back."

"You're never going to get an opportunity like this again, and you paid dearly for it."

"These people are powerful. They play rough, and they play for keeps. I won't just get a slap on the wrist if they don't want to play along."

"You can always keep going the way you are. No refunds, though."

"My ambition won't let me."

"Ambition is a hard taskmaster."

"Don't give me platitudes!"

"Then do what you know you have to do!" Tiffany hung up.

Would the DNC take the bait? Was he too subtle? Did they understand what he was offering? Were they calling his bluff? Dalton stopped pacing. Blowing the whistle on his own, albeit secret, party wouldn't help him any. He was sure the Republicans had guessed a long time ago that he wasn't much of a conservative. Maybe he could use this information to ingratiate himself with them, instead of the Democrats, if it wasn't too late. He was going to use it one way or another. He knew he'd never get another opportunity like this again, not one this valuable. It looked like he would have to spell it out for them.

He sat down in front of his laptop and tapped out a message to his contact at the DNC. When he finished, his finger hovered over the enter key. There was no going back if he sent this message. Right now, if contacted about the press conference announcement, he could still pretend it was Madison who had the information on the president. If he was transparent with his contact, his position in the Democratic organization would change. Not only would he have to publicly switch parties, but also these people were powerful and not to be trifled with.

But his career wasn't going anywhere. What was he supposed to do, sit around in this office, year after year, handing out political favors, putting up with stupid secretaries? He had ambitions; he had plans. This was the only way to do it. He hit send.

Tiffany disconnected her phone call with Dalton and continued to her car. Pulling out of the parking lot, she noticed a small black one pulled out too. She adjusted her mirror, keeping an eye on the dark car. She switched lanes and took a sudden right turn; it followed. Tiffany pulled into an alley, backed out into the street, and continued on, doubling back. As soon as the black car turned around, she hit the gas and took the first side street. She quickly parked in front of a delivery truck, hoping it would shield her when the car tailing her passed by the street. After a few minutes, when it didn't appear, she continued carefully out of the neighborhood.

Over the next few days, Maddie waited for the other shoe to drop. Was she going to be charged with a crime or not? Jay had helped her hire a lawyer to get the slow wheels of justice turning, but so far all that had happened on the senator's end was sending a termination notice for her job. The reason had been "unsatisfactory conduct." She'd frowned when she read the notice. Why was the senator being so vague? She tore it up and threw it away. Afterward, realizing she might need it, she dug the pieces out of her garbage, shaking off coffee grounds. She pieced it together and taped the coffee-stained fragments. It was like a microcosm of her life: stained, torn, and put back together, but barely. What was she going to do?

Maddie's bank account was okay so far. Her rent and school loan payments were high, but she lived pretty simply, so there was some money in the bank - some, not a lot. She was going to have to find another job soon. But who would hire her as a speechwriter? No one would trust her. It was all so unfair! She hadn't done anything wrong. Maddie prayed daily for strength and for justice to win out.

Twenty-four

Tiffany smoothed her skirt, feeling more like herself than she had in days. She'd stopped at her favorite boutique and bought an outfit that accented her curves better than stiff jeans and a University of Georgetown sweatshirt.

She had been truly frightened, but perhaps she had overreacted to the car-tailing incident. Sure, the DNC might be keeping tabs on her, but maybe that was all it was, although there was that man in her apartment... That could have been a simple robbery. Or it could have been attempted rape. She shivered, unsure if she should go back to work.

While heading to her car, she got a call on her cell. She didn't recognize the number and hesitated before answering. It went to voice mail and her phone signaled a message had been left.

It was the manager of her apartment building. In a short, tense message, he let her know that someone had broken into her apartment again. This time her place had been ransacked. The manager had changed the locks and needed her back there right away to tell the police what was missing. Maddie was instantly on edge, looking around to see if she was being followed again.

She had no intention of returning to her apartment. Her copy of the information she'd given to Dalton was still in a safety deposit box. She tried to call the senator, but the phone went immediately to voice mail without ringing.

Dalton Stanfield entered the Hart Building much later than usual and moved through the lobby almost without seeing the tourists milling around him. His head was pounding with another migraine. He pulled out his phone with shaking, sweating hands and immediately dropped it. Just as he bent over and reached for it, someone next to him kicked it across the lobby where it hit the wall. He hurried over to it. A small tow-headed boy standing by the wall picked it up and handed it to him. Dalton mumbled his thanks. Was it broken? He swiped the screen and saw that it still worked. He sighed, but he didn't feel relief. He searched through his recent texts and incoming calls to see if he'd missed something. He'd had a call from Tiffany but didn't return the call. Why contact her? She couldn't help him now.

Engrossed in his phone, he didn't notice a group of children on a tour had surrounded him and were moving en masse toward the enormous *Mountains and Clouds* sculpture. Someone bumped into him from behind, so he automatically moved forward. He was herded under the arched legs of a "mountain" with the group and was pushed into the actual sculpture. He felt the cold sheet metal against his skin and felt suffocated by the crowd. Roughly shoving the children aside, he moved quickly through the atrium.

Heading toward his office, he noticed his hands felt gummy. Turning over his phone, he saw it had a shiny spot. The kid who picked it up must have had something on his hands. "Kids! Why are they always so sticky?" he muttered and headed toward the bathroom.

When he entered, he noticed the same high-powered hand dryer was still stuck on from the last time he was in there. Would maintenance never fix that? He quickly washed his hands, wiped his phone with a piece of damp toilet paper, and hurried on to his office.

A maintenance man was working on an outlet in the hall. Dalton quickly told him about the annoying hand dryer. The worker said he'd take care of it and returned to his work. Dalton shook his head. More incompetence. He knew the man wouldn't lift a finger to do anything.

He barely acknowledged Jeanie's greeting as he entered her office.

"Here are your mail and your messages," she said handing him a pile of paperwork. He grunted and was continuing on his way.

"Also your letter opener is missing," she said.

"My letter opener!" He stared at her for a second in disbelief; then he continued into his own office, almost slamming the door in his hurry. What did he care about a stupid letter opener? The woman couldn't handle the simplest of details.

"Never mind," she said quietly to no one. "I'll take care of it."

Dalton went straight to his desk. Opening a drawer, he grabbed a bottle and shook out some pills into his hand, not noticing what kind of pain reliever it was or how many he took. He downed them with some bottled water. He collapsed on his couch, shutting his eyes. His office was too bright. He wouldn't have come in at all, but he'd left his laptop here, and he needed to check his emails to see if the Democratic National Committee had contacted him. His head was still splitting, and he was so tired.

He needed a plan if the DNC wouldn't play ball. He didn't have any inside contacts with the RNC. Whom would he contact?

Right now, he couldn't concentrate on a plan. He was so tired and his legs felt numb. He'd take just a short nap before checking his email account.

Tiffany needed to think, needed a plan. Someone had to warn Madison. Tiffany called Dalton's assistant, Jeanie, to get Madison's phone number and address, claiming they'd made a time to get together that she had to cancel. The woman gave her the information without a second thought. Dalton needed to sack that woman; Jeanie had no idea what it meant to protect confidentiality. Of course, Tiffany had been counting on that. She tried to call Madison without success; she didn't leave a message.

Leaving her car where she'd parked it, Tiffany got on the Metro. She hated public transportation. She avoided it at all cost but thought she'd be harder to tail, that she'd blend in, riding with the masses. She tried to monitor those around her on the train, but men always stared at her, so that wasn't a clue. No one following her would be obvious.

Even though the day was cool, she was sweating. Anyone on the train could shoot her or pull out a knife and stab her with a crowd like this around. She hated crowds. Why had she taken the train? It wasn't any safer here. She had to get off.

Tiffany left the Metro too early leaving herself almost a mile to walk. The GPS on her phone gave her Madison's address. The last few blocks she took a circuitous route, even cutting across through some yards. She hadn't done that since she was a kid and wouldn't be doing it again. She didn't want a homeowner to feel threatened and pull a gun on her. After all, she was trespassing. Also, her heels kept getting stuck in the soft sod though she stepped gingerly. She tried to call Dalton again. He didn't pick up. This time she left a message.

"Someone broke into my apartment! The DNC must know that I gave you the information? We're all in danger. Call me."

Maddie glared at her computer. Why should she have to update her resume already? She'd just started this job and had been so excited at the thought of living her dream, writing speeches, on her way to helping change the world. "I guess that's the bad thing about dreams. You wake up."

Her phone rang. She didn't recognize the number and didn't answer it.

She took a sip of coffee and petted Franky. He was there by her side, faithfully snuggled up in his usual spot. "You don't know how bad things are, do you boy? Just wait until there's no more puppy chow in your food bowl. Then you'll understand what 'terminated' means."

Someone knocked on the door. Franky ran to it and started barking. Maddie looked through the peephole and saw a young woman about her age. She looked like a model with long, smooth, black hair. Maddie felt like an absolute drudge just looking at her through the door. The woman looked vaguely familiar, but Maddie couldn't place her. She shut Franky in her bedroom, put on a robe, and opened the door.

The woman who stood on her steps looked uneasy. If anyone should be uneasy, Maddie thought, it should be her with no makeup and her hair in a messy ponytail standing next to the perfectly coifed woman. "May I help you?" Maddie asked.

The woman looked around outside. "My name is Tiffany Roberts. I'm Senator Reed's aide. May I come in?"

Curious, Maddie opened the door wider. Tiffany came inside and quickly closed the door. She crossed to the window, stood to the side, and looked out toward the street. Maddie looked out the window. There wasn't anyone out there. The woman struck her as a mix of chic beauty and paranoia. Somehow, it worked for her.

"Look, I won't take up your time. I know you don't know me, but I wanted to warn you about Senator Stanfield."

Maddie moved to the sofa and plopped down. "Too late. I guess you don't watch the news."

Tiffany kept her place next to the window and shook her head, her shiny hair flowing. How did she get her hair to shine that way? Maddie's always seemed dull, no matter what products she bought. She considered asking Tiffany what conditioner she used. Of course, Maddie couldn't afford anything right now with no job, so why ask? How depressing, couldn't even afford a bottle of a good conditioner. She sighed. The woman had perfect posture, too.

"No, you don't understand. He's in deeper than you could know," Tiffany said.

"No, I don't understand. Deeper into what?"

Tiffany stiffened at the window. "Is there a back way out of here?" she asked.

"Sure, the back stairs from the kitchen." Maddie pointed toward it. "What were you saying about the senator?"

But Tiffany was gone. Maddie went into the kitchen. The door stood open. Seeing no sign of Tiffany, she closed it and made sure it was locked. Then she made her way back to the front door and ensured it was locked, too. She let Franky out of the bedroom wondering what was up with that visit.

"This just keeps getting weirder and weirder."

Maddie's phone rang. She picked it up and looked at the screen to see who was calling. It was Jay. She considered not taking the call. She didn't blame him for what happened, but she didn't want to be cheered up. Maybe he had some news from the lawyer, though. Maddie answered with the speaker on and laid down on the couch.

"Hello?"

"Mad? This is Jay."

"Hi, Jay. You're on speakerphone." Maddie stuffed a pillow under her head.

"Who's there?"

"Just Franky and me... now"

Jay paused. "Okay. Well, I'll make sure I don't say anything your dog can't hear. "

"I just had a visitor, Tiffany Roberts. She's Senator Reed's aide."

"I don't know her, but he's as corrupt as they come. What did she want?"

"She said she wanted to warn me about Senator Stanfield. She said he was 'in deeper' than I could know. Then she acted like someone was after her and left by the back way."

"Really? 'In deeper'? I wonder what she meant by that. He's in pretty deep."

Maddie wasn't interested in figuring out puzzles. She sighed. "I don't have any idea what she meant. I think she was making Mission Impossible 6 and used my living room to shoot a scene."

Are you all right, Mad? You sound..."

"Crazy?" Maddie provided.

"Stressed."

"I've been updating my resume. It's depressing."

"Well, a lot of things are still up in the air. Don't give up yet."

"I guess you haven't heard from the lawyer?"

She could almost see him hesitating. "No," he finally said.

"Shouldn't I have been accused of something by now? I mean other than on national TV? Shouldn't the attorney general or someone be contacting me, charging me?" Mad sat up and took a drink of her coffee. It was cold. She drank some anyway.

"I don't think this case is something the attorney general would be involved in."

"Okay, then shouldn't the local police be showing up at my door with lights flashing and hauling me off to prison?"

"Do you want me to see if there is a warrant out for your arrest?"

"Never been asked that by a guy before. I guess so."

"Let's meet for coffee, Mad."

"Isn't that how this whole thing started?"

"No, that is how *we* started."

Maddie considered. "We, hmm, is there a 'we'?"

Jay's voice came strongly through the phone. "There is most definitely a 'we.' If you want there to be," he added.

"Are you sure you want to get involved with a criminal?"

"I'll take my chances," he said.

"Okay, I could use some coffee, but I'm not going to the Daily Grind ever again."

"Fine. I've wanted to try Ebenezer's for a while."

"Ebenezer's? Never heard of it."

"Their thing is fair trade coffee. Their motto is 'Coffee with a cause.' It's run by a church."

"Sounds good to me. I am always up for new coffeehouses. I'll need some time to get ready, though."

"It's just coffee. You don't have to get dressed up."

"I'm in my pajamas," Maddie said flatly. It was

four o'clock in the afternoon.

There was another pause. "Okay, it's probably a little more formal than that."

"Give me an hour. Do you want to meet there?"

"No, I'll come pick you up."

"Afraid to let me out loose on the streets of D.C. behind the wheel of a car?"

"Something like that."

Maddie yawned. "Okay, since I don't have to drive anywhere, I can be ready in 45 minutes."

"Okay. I'll be there. Bye."

"Bye." Maddie looked at her screen. Her phone was almost dead. She turned it off, went into her bedroom, and plugged it into the charger on her nightstand. It should be charged enough by the time she was ready to go since she'd turned it off.

She returned to the living room to find Franky balanced half on the couch and half on the coffee table with his long nose in her mug lapping up the remains of her cold coffee. At least he hadn't spilled it this time. He was getting better at it. She shooed him away and took the cup in the kitchen to rinse it out, and then headed to the bathroom for a shower.

Franky followed her into the bedroom and jumped up on the bed. "Naptime again, huh, fella? I wouldn't think you'd be able to sleep after your cup of java." He rearranged the covers and curled up in a ball.

Tiffany had to get to her car. She hated to do it

but made her way through the neighborhood using backyards rather than going the other way, knowing she'd be readily seen if using the sidewalks. She wasn't taking a chance with that black car that had been following her. It took a long time to cross all of those muddy yards. If only she was still wearing the jeans, T-shirt, and low heels she'd been wearing all week. She finally removed her shoes and went barefoot. She reached a Metro station and quickly got on the train. Not used to taking the subway, she misjudged which stop to get off at and had to backtrack to reach her car.

With all of the different routes taken, she must have lost the tail. After stopping to buy a couple of changes of clothes, Tiffany wanted nothing more than to soak away her troubles and sore feet in a tub. She decided to stay at a hotel this time, not willing to endanger McKenzie or her sister by staying at the university. She picked a place as far away as possible from her apartment and everyone she knew and checked in, leaving her car in the parking lot of the hotel next door. On the way to her room, she called Kate and asked her to pick up Ebony from McKenzie, being vague about the reason why.

When she reached her room, Mitch called. She couldn't put him off again.

"Dinner tonight?" he asked. He certainly was persistent.

"Sure, I'll need some time to get ready, though." She went into the bathroom and scrubbed the mud off her shoes.

"We could meet at La Maison Belle," Mitch

said.

"How about Salvatore's?" she suggested.

"Okay, where is it?"

"It's kind of far out, almost to Virginia," she said.

He paused. "Okay, if that's where you want to eat, I'll find it with my GPS."

"Good. 7 o'clock?"

"See you at 7," he said.

What a relief it was not to have to show up in the heart of D.C. with all that had been happening to her. She was going to have to catch Mitch up on a few things. Then she was going to have to break his   heart.

Twenty-five

There was a knock on the door. Dalton stirred. Jeanie stuck her head in and had to look behind the door to find him on the couch. "I'm sorry to bother you. I didn't know you were asleep. I just wanted to let you know I'm leaving for the day."

Dalton grunted a goodbye and watched Jeanie close the door. He tried to rise from the couch, but he felt very groggy, and he still had a headache. He wondered what kind of pain reliever he'd taken. He stumbled to his desk and found the bottle. "Sleeping pills! I thought it was aspirin. Where did those come from?" He'd taken several, too.

He dropped into the chair in front of his laptop and tried to remember which password he used to log onto his computer. He finally remembered, but he struggled to focus on the screen. He opened his email account. There was an email from his DNC contact! It listed a complicated message in code about where to meet. He hit reply and told him he'd be there. He staggered back to the couch and fell onto it again. He'd figure the meeting place from the message later. Right now, he needed a little more sleep.

Maddie came out of the bathroom to find that a glass of water on the nightstand had tipped over and spilled on her charging phone. She grabbed it and looked around for the culprit. "Franky!" she shrieked. Franky did not come. Maddie went looking for him and found him cowering in the kitchen. "You ruined my phone!" she said. "There's no money for a new phone, Franky." She was about to turn it on to see if it worked when she remembered she'd heard that if a cell phone gets wet, it shouldn't be turned on right away. It should be dried off and put in a bowl of rice to absorb the moisture. Maddie quickly took her phone apart, removed the battery, and dried all of the pieces with paper towels. She emptied a bag of rice into a small mixing bowl and buried the phone in it.

Just as she was finishing, there was a knock at the door. She hurried into the living room. Jay was right on time, but she'd spent so much time trying to save her phone, she wasn't ready yet. She checked to make sure it was Jay before she opened the door. There he stood, looking good as usual, while she was running around in a bathrobe, with her hair in a towel and no makeup. She almost ran from the room after she let him in. Would he ever see her at her best rather than her worst?

Tiffany rued making the date for 7 o'clock. She would have loved to soak in the tub for another hour. She dragged herself out and put on one of the dresses she'd bought. It wasn't from her usual shop, but it still looked good, and the price was right. She eyed her shoes, not willing to stuff her tender, swollen feet into them. She did it anyway and knew she couldn't spend the evening in those heels. She made her way to the gift shop on the ground floor and bought a pair of sandals that didn't hurt as much.

Tiffany exited the hotel, looking around carefully, and headed for her car. It was quite a trek with her sore feet. She was so glad to be able to sit down on the car seat. She drove to Salvatore's, arriving early, and parked in the farthest space from the entrance. She sat there for several minutes looking around. The restaurant was Italian with torches lighting up the outside deck and the entrance. It looked like a nice place. Too bad, she probably wouldn't get anything to eat since Mitch would no doubt leave when he heard her out. She didn't think she had been followed. She finally went inside, dreading the evening and the conversation that was about to take place.

When Mad ran from the room, Jay called after her, "I've seen you looking much worse you know."

"Trying to cheer me up? Franky dumped water on my phone."

"Take your phone apart and put it in rice. It absorbs the moisture."

"I already did that," she called from the bedroom. "I need coffee."

"That's the story of your life," he called back.

"You don't know the half of it," she said as she emerged from the other room. She got ready pretty fast for a woman. She looked good, too, although her hair was still wet. She was scrunching it with her fingers and grabbed her purse. "Let's go," she said. So much for cheering her up. He followed her out the door. Jay hoped good coffee would lighten her mood.

Mitch arrived right on time and joined Tiffany at the table. He greeted her with his usual kiss on the cheek and a smile. Tiffany wanted to echo his smile, but she couldn't.

"My apartment was broken into again, ransacked this time," she said.

"Ransacked? What were they after? Jewelry? Electronics? Tell me you weren't staying there."

"No, I've been staying with a friend. And I'd have to guess what's missing since I haven't been back to check it out." Tiffany knew this was the opening she needed. She drew a deep breath. "I think they were looking for a copy of some documents that have come into my possession."

"Documents? You mean for work?" he asked sipping from the glass of water the waiter had dropped off.

"No. These documents were confidential, having to do with inside information gathered on a high-level politician," she said.

Mitch looked grave. "How did they come into your possession?" he asked quietly.

"It doesn't matter," she said softly. "Politics makes strange bedfellows. What's important is that this is the life I lead."

"You mean this is your job," he said.

"No, I mean it is my life. I chose this, knowing

how D.C. operates. Try to understand. This city rules the country. This city is America. Everything else that happens doesn't matter except in how it relates to Washington D.C. Working in politics in the Capitol is like the difference between playing baseball in the major leagues..."

"Or the minors?" he asked.

"Or pee wee ball," she finished.

"Do you believe in fate?" he said.

"That's quite a change in topics," Tiffany said lightly, remembering how her sister had suggested the very same idea, that fate had taken a hand. "Have you been talking to Kate?"

"Kate? No, when I ran into you while I was jogging along the river, my plane had just landed that day. I was planning to look you up, and you practically fell into my lap!" He sounded so happy; it hurt her to hear it. Yet she couldn't look away, and she couldn't steer the conversation from the inevitable one.

"Mitch, about that day." She paused, and then purposefully went on. "If you knew what I had just done..."

He took her hands. "I don't care. I know that people involved in politics have to sometimes do things that are somewhat... unethical." Tiffany could see it pained him to say the word in context with her. "But I'm sure you haven't done anything wrong."

Tiffany pulled her hands away. "What I've done, I did because it had to be done."

Mitch paused. "You always had integrity..."

Tiffany shook her head. "I was a child. The

worst thing I did in Tekoa was booby-trap the dunking tank. I've had to... adapt. This city runs on power. Once you get on to ride that train, you don't get off until it comes to the end of the line."

"What's at the end of the line, Tiff? Jail... or worse?"

"You don't find out until the train reaches the station, Mitch," she said softly.

Mitch looked away. It was the only time she could remember him doing that. Tiffany didn't say anything for a few seconds. If she blinked, the tears would overflow. She withdrew her hands and took a drink of water.

When Dalton awoke, he noticed it was already growing dark. He forced himself to rise. He stretched, found a Starbucks double shot in his mini-fridge, and drank it down in just a few gulps. He slumped in the chair in front of his laptop. He was still feeling groggy, but he could concentrate a little better. He looked at the message he'd left open on his laptop. He could figure it out, now. He was instructed to meet someone at the Lincoln Memorial. He wondered if he would be meeting Darrell Washburn himself. That was probably too risky, for Washburn though. There were cameras everywhere at the monument.

He was about to delete the message as instructed when he noticed it warned him not to tell anyone about the meeting or the message. A chill passed through him as he realized he could be making a very risky move, a deadly one. What was to stop them from just eliminating him? He tried to think of someone he could forward the email to that he could trust in case something happened to him. It was in code anyway. He'd have to decipher it. But there wasn't anyone. Dalton had no one close enough to him to trust with something as sensitive and potentially damaging as this. All he had were superficial acquaintances. He gave a short, bitter laugh. Networkers, that was all he had. People who would advance his career.

Since he'd included Madison in his scheme, she could be in danger, too. When he'd contacted the DNC for help with her, they'd sent him that ridiculous hacker. They'd also immediately started having Clark and Madison followed. Dalton had heard the DNC had many unsavory characters on their payroll. He shuddered as he suddenly saw he'd put himself, Madison, and Clark in grave danger. Yes, she'd turned on him and given secret information to Clark, but Dalton didn't want her killed. Maybe he should warn her. He could forward the email to her.

He shook himself and took a deep breath. Where was his head? Those sleeping pills were keeping him from thinking clearly. That big mouth Clark would have this spread over the entire country within 24 hours. He couldn't give this information to Madison. Dalton deleted the message.

At least the meeting was scheduled in a public place. What could happen in the Lincoln Memorial?

Twenty-six

Jay and Mad took their coffees to a couple of comfy chairs in front of a window. The brick and the rust-colored interior felt warm and inviting. Mad had already tried her latte and commented on how good it was, although it was too hot to drink. It looked like this would be a good substitute for the Daily Grind, especially since there were no bad memories associated with it. They moved their chairs so the setting sun hit them but wasn't in their eyes. Mad set her purse beside her on the chair and started scrunching her damp hair again as she had the whole way there in the car.

"Did you call the police?" Mad asked quietly, shielding her mouth with her hand as though someone nearby could read her lips.

Jay nodded. "There is no warrant out for your arrest."

"But he could still accuse me of it, couldn't he? I mean, I could have this hanging over me for the rest of my life."

Jay shook his head. "I don't think so, Mad. I think he's up to something else. Politicians don't want negative publicity. If he had a speechwriter who did what he's accused you of, the normal course of action would be to fire the writer quietly. No, I think the fact that he called a press conference and announced it means he's using this for another purpose."

"How could he use this?"

"I have been asking myself that question. I

have no idea." Jay admitted.

Mad tried to take a sip of her coffee. "Still too hot."

"Why do you order it extra hot? You can't drink it until it cools anyway."

Mad stretched her legs. "If it starts out lukewarm, it's too cold right away."

"Have you sent out any resumes yet?" Jay tried to sound like he didn't dread the answer.

"Not yet, I'm still updating it. I'm trying to find a euphemism for 'fired.' 'Laid off' isn't true. 'Sacked' sounds flippant. 'Dismissed' has a little dignity at least."

"'Let go'?" Jay suggested.

"I don't know," Mad took another sip. "Even though I've lost my job and my reputation is ruined, at least there is still good coffee."

"And there are still people who care about you. One is sitting here right now." Jay knew this probably wasn't the right time to talk about this, but when would be a good time? After she moved to another state?

Mad looked at him over the top of her coffee mug but didn't say anything.

"Look, Mad, I know we got off to a rough start, but I want you to know you can count on me. I'm going to help as much as I can to get your name cleared." Jay put his hand on her arm that wasn't holding the coffee. "I care about you."

Mad still didn't say anything, but her eyes filled with tears.

Jay patted her leg. "It's okay, Mad. We can talk about this later. Are you getting hungry?"

She nodded. "I forgot to eat lunch."

Jay was about to suggest they try The Kitchen again, but he didn't want to upset Mad further with a bad memory. It was good there were so many restaurants available in D.C. "Where would you like to eat? What do you feel like?"

"I feel like I'm bad news, bad for your career," she said.

"And that's a bad pun," said Jay. "You're hungry. You'll feel better after you have something to eat."

"Tiffany... why didn't I think of her before? She's in this as deep as I am. I could have sent her the message." Dalton blamed his inability to concentrate on the grogginess from the pills. He had a few minutes until he had to leave to meet his contact at the Lincoln Memorial. He looked back over his call log and figured out her number.

His call went straight to voice mail. Her sultry voice came on the line. "This is Tiffany; you know what to do."

"Tiffany, this is Dalton... Stanfield. I'm meeting someone from the DNC at the Lincoln Memorial at 9:00." He hesitated. What else should he say? Warn her? Ask her to be his backup? Tiffany was an up-and-coming female version of himself. A networker, no more. He couldn't count on her for help any more than anyone else. "Watch yourself," he said grimly and hung up.

Tiffany's phone rang. She ignored it. She couldn't have spoken if she had answered the call.

Mitch wouldn't look at her. It was more devastating than anything she would see in his eyes. To know that he was disappointed in her made her heartsick.

Tiffany could barely choke out the word "goodbye." She gathered her things and turned to go. Her phone signaled a nofication. She walked away from the table listening to the voice mail Dalton left. She was surprised at the message and frankly puzzled. It didn't seem like he'd listened to her message at all. Anyway, what did he expect her to do? Hide at the Lincoln Memorial in the shadows with a gun and pick off anyone who threatened him? Having no intention of skulking around the monument in the dark, she hung up her phone.

Maddie carried her coffee as Jay took her other arm and lightly steered her toward the door. He was very sweet. His behavior reminded her of the protective way men seemed to naturally treat women in the black and white movies she loved. She could tell he liked her, and she felt the same way, but she didn't want to ruin his life and career by dating him. Just associating with her could make him look corrupt, too. They should back off, at least for a while, after tonight until things smoothed out.

As he held the door for her, she remembered they'd met not from the coffee spill, but from him getting the door at The Daily Grind. The simple act of a door held open to enter a coffee shop caused him to enter her life. Now, the same gesture as they exited another one, signified her exit from his life. They stepped out into the growing dark of the early evening, and Maddie felt a sadness at the thought of losing him and all he'd come to mean to her. But it would be selfish to continue the relationship.

As they crossed the street to Jay's car, Maddie suddenly realized she'd left her purse in her chair in Ebenezer's. She stopped, grabbed Jay's arm, and turned, pulling him along with her. "I forgot my..."

Before she could say what she forgot, a car came careening down the middle of the street where Maddie and Jay had stood a second earlier, just missing them, and then sped away! Jay grabbed Maddie and pulled her onto the sidewalk. He held her close. "Are you all right?"

Shaken, she couldn't say anything.

He put his arm around her while he led her back into the coffeehouse and over to the seats they had just left. She dropped into the chair, grabbed her purse, and hugged it to her. "This purse saved our lives!" she said.

Jay knelt before her and took her hand. "Thank God you forgot it. We'd both be dead right now."

"My klutziness actually helped for once," Maddie said ruefully.

Jay tipped Maddie's chin up and looked her in the eye." You are not a klutz. You are a beautiful woman who has had a few bad experiences. And what you term 'klutziness' brought you to me."

"Yes, well, the jury's still out on that one," Maddie tried to stand. Jay helped her.

"Where's your coffee?" Jay looked around.

"I must have dropped it outside. Boy, it just kills me the way some people drive!"

"I think that was the idea," Jay said as they left Ebenezer's again. He looked around.

"What do you mean?"

"I don't think that was just bad driving. Lately, everywhere we go, I've seen a little black car like that one that just tried to run us down." Maddie and Jay crossed the street and got into his car.

"There are a lot of little black cars, Jay."

"Well, it was parked outside your house a few nights ago, and when I approached it, it sped off... twice."

"That could be anything."

"Yes, or it could be someone is trying to hurt you." Jay looked carefully before he pulled out into traffic. "Where do you want to go to eat?"

"Oh, I couldn't eat anything now. I'm too upset. Could you just take me home?" Maddie still clutched her purse to her.

Jay pulled over. He turned to her. "I think you should spend the night at my condo tonight."

"Excuse me?" Maddie whipped her head around and looked at Jay.

"I don't mean it like that! I think someone is trying to kill you!"

"My parents will kill me if I spend the night at your place. I'm sure it was just careless driving. Everyone drives crazy in this town."

"Well, I'd feel better if you stayed at my condo." Jay pulled into traffic again.

"No way. What would your neighbors think?"

"I don't care what my neighbors think. I care

about you!"

"Well, I think you're overreacting, and I am not staying at your condo," Maddie asserted.

"Then, how about I sleep on your couch tonight?"

"Oh, my landlady would love that? Besides, I have Franky to protect me."

"Oh, he's a big help. What would he do, trip him or lick him to death?"

"I was thinking he would bark and let me know someone was lurking about my apartment."

Jay pulled into Maddie's driveway. He got out, opened the door for her, and followed her up the stairs, looking all around.

Maddie stopped outside. "Look, Jay. I lock my door as soon as I walk through it. All of my windows are locked. I have Franky. You don't have anything to worry about. I'll be fine."

Jay put his arms around her and pulled her close. "I don't know what I'd do if something happened to you."

"Nothing's going to happen. I'll be fine," she repeated.

She was about to tell him that she'd decided they shouldn't see each other for a while when he leaned forward and kissed her. It was much longer than the "forgotten" kiss. She didn't remember until after he was already down the steps that she wasn't planning to see him anymore.

"Call me if you need me. I'm not far," Jay called over his shoulder as he walked away.

Twenty-seven

As Tiffany left the restaurant, Mitch ran to catch up with her. He stopped her on the deck next to a torch. The light from the torch backlit her, ringing her with a soft glow. He surrounded her with an embrace that held all of the words he hadn't uttered. The depth of his love, the years of waiting, the forgiveness. Tiffany received it, but she knew it wouldn't change the outcome.

She kissed him on the cheek and started to pull away. She caught a glimpse of someone approaching, pulling a gun from within his jacket!

Mitch must have seen it too. He quickly pushed her to the ground and shielded her with his body. She barely heard the muffled shots, but she felt Mitch fall heavily next to her! Panicked, she quickly squeezed under the deck and hid beneath the stairs. She heard footsteps nearby. Holding her breath as she looked between the stairs, she could see two men roll Mitch over. One of them stood right by her. If he moved a couple of inches forward, he would kick her with his green Converse high tops. She moved back, slowly and quietly.

"Yeah, he's dead," one of them said. Tiffany almost gasped. She put her hand over her mouth.

"Where did the girl go? She's the one we were supposed to get."

"She must have run off. Maybe she went back inside. We'll have to check the area."

"We don't have time for that. We still have to

get over to McPherson's."

"Let's split up. What about the senator?" Tiffany didn't hear the answer. The men climbed into a black car and left. She rolled out from under the deck and raced to her car calling the police while she ran. She had to warn Madison and Dalton! She would call Dalton immediately after she summoned the police and ambulance.

It was dark by the time Dalton grabbed his briefcase and left his office. There was one more thing he needed to do before he left for the night. Jeanie kept a log of visitors. He pulled it out of her desk and leafed through it. Reaching the page with "John Smith" and Madison's entries, he carefully pulled it out and ran it through the shredder. He'd talk to Jeanie tomorrow about her breach of security by not locking her desk.

There was nobody in the hall except the maintenance man he'd told about the dryer. He was still working on the outlet. Typical bureaucratic incompetence, thought Dalton, taking as long as possible to do a simple job.

The man approached him, now. "Uh, Senator, could you give me a hand with that dryer?"

Dalton looked at his watch. He barely had time to make it to the rendezvous site as it was. If he missed this meeting... He sighed.

"It shouldn't take long," said the maintenance man. Dalton led the way to the restroom. His phone started to ring. He hit ignore.

Tiffany had directed the 9-1-1 dispatcher to

Salvatore's. They wanted her to stay on the line, but she told them someone's life was at stake and disconnected the call without waiting for permission. When she called Dalton, she was sent to his voice mail. Her call to Madison went unanswered, too. Fortunately, she still remembered the address. She needed to let Madison know she was in danger and warn Dalton the DNC had sent men to kill him. She tried his phone again. He didn't pick up, so she sent him a text.

When she arrived at Madison's house, it was dark. She knocked, but there was no one home. She scribbled a note and pushed it under the door.

Since she had no other way to contact Dalton, she had to get to the Lincoln Memorial before he met his contact from the DNC and warn him that the men were trying to kill him. The realization of Mitch's death was overwhelming her, but she got in her car and headed toward the monument, trying not to think about the horror of what had taken place at Salvatore's.

The dryer was already running when the senator and the maintenance man entered the restroom. The maintenance guy set his toolbox down on the floor and opened it. Dalton gestured to the dryer and started to leave. It suddenly occurred to him that he hadn't ever seen maintenance staff stay this late to do repair work before.

He turned around just as the man moved toward him with something that looked like a knife raised in his hand! Dalton smashed his briefcase into the man's head. He staggered, but it didn't stop him. He came at Dalton again. Dalton hit the arm holding the knife with the briefcase. The knife went flying. The attacker grunted and lunged for the knife. Dalton tried to get to the door, but the man found the knife and came at him again. As Dalton raised his briefcase to shield himself, he saw it wasn't a knife but a letter opener. It glanced off the case and sliced Dalton's arm. He yelled in pain. The man raised the letter opener again. Dalton hit the man's hand again with his briefcase, knocking the letter opener under the stall door into the corner. The man turned around and grabbed something from the toolbox while Dalton raced toward the door. Before he could get it open, he felt something stab him in the back. He arched his back and then crumpled in a heap beside the toolbox, the razor-sharp screwdriver that had pierced his back lay beside him. The man leaned over him, his hands on his knees, panting. Weakened, Dalton grabbed the first thing his hand came to in the toolbox, a box cutter, and reaching up in one movement sliced the man in the throat.

There was a look of surprise on the man's face as he collapsed next to him, spraying him with blood. Dalton tried to crawl to the door, but it was blocked with the man's body. Exhausted, he pulled out his phone. He called 911, giving his location. The dispatcher wanted to keep him on the phone until help came, but feeling his life ebbing out of him, there was something Dalton had to do before it was too late.

Tearing through the streets of D.C., Tiffany tried to be strong but couldn't hold back the tears. Racked with sobs, she could barely see to drive. Mitch was gone! Mitch was dead! Why was it the innocent ones who suffered? He had saved her life by blocking the bullet meant for her.

Stalled by a stoplight, Tiffany squeezed the steering wheel, tears still falling. She was tempted to run the light to get to her destination in time but knew if stopped by a cop that she'd never get to the Lincoln   Memorial   in   time.

Twenty-eight

As Maddie let Franky out for the last time that night, she looked around from the safety of her doorstep but didn't see a black car or anyone lurking about. Being a reporter, Jay would hear terrible stories all the time and get used to assuming the worst. She would continue to be cautious as always but not paranoid.

Franky was taking unusually long. Maddie peered into the darkness but couldn't see him. "Franky!" He didn't come. "Franky, what is taking you so long?"

She stepped onto the landing and looked toward the front of the street. She didn't see her dachshund but did see Jay's car parked in her driveway!

She marched down the stairs and over to the car. He was writing on a yellow legal pad. She knocked on the window. Jay looked sheepish as he rolled it down.

"Just what do you think you are doing in my driveway?"

Jay got out of the car. "I am protecting you!"

"I had no idea you were so stubborn! I don't need protecting!"

"Well, I think you do, and I am not leaving you alone tonight!"

"Do you realize that my landlady cannot see into your car? She probably thinks you are in my apartment!"

Jay looked around. "Well, no, that hadn't

occurred to me."

"Well, it will occur to her! I will not have her thinking I have men spend the night. Now please leave!" Maddie strode back to the steps. Franky came running, tail wagging. She picked him up and carried him upstairs. She stood on the landing until she saw Jay pull out of the driveway.

She went into her apartment and put Franky on the floor. He jumped up on the couch and curled up in his usual place on the afghan, chewing on something. Maddie pulled it out of his mouth. Yuck! It was a soggy, chewed-up piece of paper. She tossed it in the garbage can, did a few dishes, and straightened up her apartment. She checked every door and window to make sure they were locked and went into the bathroom to get ready for bed.

When she lay down, she noticed Franky was not in bed. Usually, he followed her into the bedroom and was already in bed when she came out of the bathroom. "Franky!" she called. He didn't come. Maddie got up and went to look for him. "Why are you playing hard-to-get the one night I want you nearby to protect me?" She found him asleep on the couch. "Come on, boy, time for bed," she called.

He didn't come, so she picked him up. He didn't wake, and he was limp in her arms like a rag doll! She put him back on the couch and shook him, calling to him but couldn't wake him. She ran for her phone to call the vet when she remembered it was still in the bowl of rice. No phone! She decided to look up the address of an emergency vet clinic in the phone book and just drive there. It was about a mile from her apartment.

"Why did I send Jay home?" she said miserably. She could use a helping hand right now. She wrapped the afghan around Franky and grabbed her purse. She carried her bundle carefully down the steps and was about to get in her car when she noticed Jay was parked in front of the house next door. She hurried over and knocked again. Jay rolled down the window.

"Something's wrong with Franky!" she cried. "I have to get him to a vet!" Jay helped her get in his car and followed her directions to the vet clinic. The whole way there, Maddie kept talking to Franky and shaking him, but he still wouldn't wake up.

When they arrived, a technician took them immediately to an examining room where a vet quickly looked Franky over. "This dog's been drugged. We'll have to pump his stomach," she stated.

"Is he going to be all right?" Maddie asked.

"The sooner we get his stomach pumped, the less effect whatever he ate will have on him. You'll need to wait in the reception area."

The vet's professional behavior made Maddie feel better. Just knowing someone was helping Franky calmed her a little. The vet tech handed the afghan to Maddie. She clutched it to herself as Jay took her hand and led her to a chair in the waiting room.

"Drugged?" Maddie said. "Who would drug my dog?"

"Do you have any neighbors who dislike Frank?" Jay asked.

She shook her head. "He and the cat next door have got into it a couple of times, but I don't think my neighbors hate Frank so much that they would drug him."

"Well, we'll know more when they examine the contents of his stomach," Jay said. "Max had food poisoning once, and they pumped his stomach. Then they looked at the contents to figure out what caused the food poisoning."

"You and Max seem pretty close," Maddie said.

"We grew up together. I don't have any brothers or sisters, and with my parents living overseas, I don't have close family around. My parents are missionaries to Colombia, South America."

"Oh, did you grow up on the mission field?" Maddie asked.

"No, my parents took an early retirement, and this is how they're spending their retirement years."

"That's cool."

"How about you? You've mentioned you have a sister, Liz."

"I don't have any other siblings," she said.

'What about your parents, Mad? Are they horrible, dead, divorced? You don't seem to want to talk about them." Jay put his arm around Maddie. She leaned her head on his shoulder.

"Do they have to be one of those?"

"You never mention them."

"My parents don't agree with the life choices I've made."

"I knew it! You have skeletons in your closet I don't know about," he teased.

"No, it's just that my dad wanted me to get a business degree or go into law or medicine. Something he called 'more marketable.'"

"So it's not enough that you're following your dream?"

Maddie looked up at him. "My dream? I've never told you anything about my dreams."

"It's clear that you love writing speeches. You put so much into them."

"I do love writing. And I wanted my writing to be a part of helping to make this country greater, by conveying great thoughts of great people."

"Like Reagan? I noticed you quoted him in a recent speech."

Maddie smiled ruefully. "Exactly, except I was hired by the antithesis of Reagan." She laid her head back down on his shoulder. "Thank you for camping outside my door and for being there for me," she said.

Jay held up his hands. "I don't know what you're talking about. I was parked in front of the Jones's house minding my own business."

Maddie smiled, "Jones? Is that their name?"

"Probably," Jay said. "You know what would make a good book? Great speeches of great people."

"Yeah, that'd be... great. Thank you for distracting me to keep my mind off Franky."

"I'm sure he's going to be all right."

Maddie sat up. "Really? Because the vet didn't seem to be sure. Did you notice she wouldn't tell me that when I asked her?"

"I'm sure she was just in a hurry to get working on him. He's going to be fine."

"You're very comforting." Maddie lay her head back on his shoulder.

"Isn't that what every guy wants to hear? Right after 'Let's just be friends.' 'You're so comforting, just like my grandmother's quilt,' Jay mocked in a falsetto.

Maddie laughed. "It's an afghan, not a quilt." She snuggled closer to Jay who wrapped his other arm around her. "Anyway, I'm glad you're here."

"And I'm not going anywhere if that's what you're thinking."

Maddie sat up and looked at him in surprise. He'd read her mind.

"I can tell you're thinking you're no good for me, Mad. That you're ruining my career."

"Well, I hadn't really termed it as 'I'm no good for you,'" Maddie said, a little indignantly. "But yes, I am ruining your career."

"Let me worry about my career. We aren't even going to discuss this. I know we started off wrong, but I think we both know that we work."

Maddie smiled. "We do? We work? Because I am currently out of a job."

Jay pulled her close. "Don't be so literal."

"I'm a writer."

"That makes you literary. I said, 'Don't be literal,'" Jay said.

"Oh, yeah. I'm so tired. I can't think. Either

way, it comes down to words," she said and laid her head back on his shoulder.

"I love words," Jay said.

"Me, too," said Maddie.

"I love you," Jay said softly.

"Me, too," said Maddie.

"So when are you going to start on that book of speeches?"

Twenty-nine

Tiffany sat in her car waiting. She'd tried to pick a spot to intercept Dalton before he reached the memorial. It was already after nine. She tried again to reach Dalton on his cell, but the call went to voice mail without him picking up. Maybe he was still at the office.

She started her car and drove to the Hart Senate Office building, but it was after hours. She tried to call him again. Dalton could be anywhere. Giving up, she decided to drive to Madison's place.

Tiffany was about to leave the parking lot where she sat outside the senate building when suddenly police cars came screaming up. Within a few minutes, it was surrounded by police, fire engines, and ambulances, completely cordoned off. Helicopters flew overhead. A news van pulled up. Grateful she was on the outskirts of the commotion rather than in the middle of it, she tried to look up the news on her phone. All she could gather was that there had been an act of violence; there was no further information.

Her phone rang. It was McKenzie, the intern she'd stayed with.

"Did you see the news, Tiffany? Did you see what's happening at work?"

"I'm in front of the building right now! All I could find out was that there was some type of altercation at Hart."

"Well, I was in a class when my professor got a call. One of the senators has been attacked."

Tiffany's felt sick. "Who was it?"

"Not only attacked but killed," she said. McKenzie always went for the drama.

"Who was killed?" Tiffany closed her eyes.

"He was stabbed!" This was excruciating. How long was McKenzie going to draw this out?

"Do you know or not, McKenzie?" Tiffany asked.

"It was Senator Stanfield," she said.

McKenzie prattled on with some other details that were lost on Tiffany. She interrupted McKenzie and got off the phone.

She watched as several paramedics wheeled out two bodies in body bags on gurneys. The words of Sir Walter Scott came to her mind. "And doubly dying, shall go down to the vile dust, from whence he sprung, unwept, unhonor'd, and unsung."

She turned on her car and started for Madison's house.

Jay and Maddie pulled into her driveway. "I wish I could have brought Franky home. I'd feel better if I could just hold him." Maddie said wistfully. Jay opened the car door for her. She grabbed her purse and the afghan, which could probably use a good washing now.

"The vet said you could pick him up tomorrow. They want to observe him overnight," Jay reminded her.

"He just looked so helpless and sad when I said goodbye." Maddie started for the steps.

"I think we should make sure there isn't any

more meat laced with ground-up sleeping pills like the vet found in Franky's stomach. What if some other dog eats it?" Jay said and pulled a high-powered flashlight from his trunk. "Which direction did he come from the last time he went out?"

Maddie sighed helplessly. "I don't know. I was so upset seeing you parked in my driveway that I didn't notice."

"Does he have a spot where he usually goes to the bathroom?" Jay asked.

"Yuck. Yes, he goes under that stand of trees." They walked toward it, Jay sweeping his flashlight in front of them.

"I see something."

"Me too, something white."

Jay focused his flashlight at the base of the tree.

"Oh no! It's that cat - the one Franky chases!" Maddie knelt to see if it was still alive. The cat moved a little.

"It must have eaten some of the poisonous meat. Where does it live?" Jay asked. Handing the flashlight to Maddie, he scooped up the cat.

"Right there!" Maddie pointed with the flashlight to a small house next door, similar to her own. They ran to it, and Maddie rang the doorbell and pounded on the door. The sleepy, indignant older woman who answered was instantly replaced with a quivering, sobbing one, once she saw her beloved pet in such a condition.

"Snowball! What happened to my baby?" She snatched the cat out of Jay's arms and screamed for her husband who came running, pulling his pants on over his boxers.

"Someone drugged my dog, and we found Snowball while we were looking for the poison. You need to get Snowball's stomach pumped right away."

"Poisoned? Henry, get the car! We have to get Snowball to a vet!" Maddie gave them the address and directions to the emergency vet clinic they had just used, and soon the couple was speeding down the road.

Maddie and Jay resumed looking for the tainted meat. They discovered it about a yard from where they'd found the cat. "There isn't much here. Franky and the cat must have eaten most of it," Jay said. "Let's get some paper towels to pick it up with."

Maddie was looking around in the dark, trying to orient herself, so she could find the spot again. Suddenly, she slid. "Eww! I think I stepped in something!" she said.

"Well, it's dark out. One of us was bound to," Jay said.

"It's fitting that it was I who did since I'm the one who didn't clean up my dog's mess. Oh well, another pair of shoes bites the dust." Maddie grimaced and tried to scrape off her shoes in the grass as they walked toward the house.

"Maybe you'll be able to clean them off," Jay offered.

"Maybe," Maddie said doubtfully.

"If you'll give me a couple of plastic bags, I'll pick up the meat," Jay offered.

When she reached the stairs, she handed the

flashlight to Jay, tucked her afghan under her arm, and took off her shoes. When would this ever end? Her shoes stunk! She scrunched up her face and held the shoes away from her as she climbed the stairs, dropping the offending things outside. She pulled out her keys and unlocked the door.

Maddie entered her apartment, dropped the afghan and her purse on the floor, and flipped the switch for the light. It didn't turn on. Thinking that was odd since there hadn't been a storm to knock out the electricity, she turned to ask Jay for the flashlight when she heard something in the corner. Someone grabbed her! Immediately, a damp cloth with a sickeningly sweet smell covered her mouth and nose, keeping her from making more than a muffled sound. Struggling to keep from breathing in, she writhed, trying to break free but couldn't. She managed to move the cloth enough to bite the hand holding it, hard. The man holding her grunted in pain but didn't release her. She screamed, "Help! Jay!"

"Maddie!"

Jay jumped into the struggle. It was almost totally black inside the apartment. The assailant released Maddie and started landing punches on Jay.

"Maddie, get out of the way!" Jay called. She backed against the wall, so he wouldn't end up hitting her.

"Bash him over the head with something!" yelled Jay, but Maddie couldn't tell in the dark which was Jay and which was the intruder. She was afraid to start swinging something in the dark.

She searched until she found the flashlight by the door and shined it in the direction of the scuffle, right into Jay's eyes! Momentarily blinded, Jay tried to block the beam with his hands. The attacker landed a blow to Jay's stomach that knocked the breath out of him. He crumpled to the floor.

Since she could see now, Maddie smacked the intruder over the head with the flashlight. It went out. The attacker got up somewhat dazedly and headed for her. She beat at him with the flashlight. He ran for the door, bumping into the doorway on his way out. Maddie threw the afghan over his head as he ran through the doorway.

Thirty

Tiffany pulled into Madison's driveway. Although the lights were off in the apartment, Tiffany could see Madison and a man walking up the steps. She parked and started toward the house.

As she was walking up the stairs, she heard a scuffle inside. The door opened and a man tried to run out of the apartment. As he was coming through the door, Tiffany could see Maddie throw some type of blanket over him.

When Maddie saw Tiffany on the stairs, she yelled, "Look out, Tiffany!"

The attacker slipped on Maddie's soiled shoes and slid a little. From Tiffany's vantage point on the stairs, she was eye level with a pair of green Converse high tops. Tiffany reached up and yanked on one of his legs. He came tumbling down the stairs head over foot and landed in a heap at the bottom, not moving.

Maddie stepped out on the landing. She heard sirens in the distance. Jay slowly joined her. "I'll bet when she heard the noise begin, my landlady called the police." Maddie noticed that Jay seemed to be in pain. "Jay are you all right?"

Jay winced. "I'm fine, just a little knocked around." Jay took her hand and cautiously led her down the stairs to join Tiffany as the police pulled into the driveway. They approached the attacker who looked like he was either dead or out cold. One of the officers shined a flashlight in his eyes and felt for a pulse. "He's alive," he said and radioed for an ambulance.

"Who lives here?" a policeman asked Maddie and Jay.

"I do." Maddie raised her hand. "And Mrs. Gustafson lives downstairs." Maddie could see her landlady timidly peeking through the curtains.

"Did you know your assailant?" the officer asked. Maddie and Jay leaned over the unconscious man.

"Isn't he the guy from the restaurant who had the Caesar salad spilled on him?" Jay asked.

"Serves him right. He must have been following me even then," Maddie said. She sat on the steps suddenly exhausted and looked up at the officer. "I didn't know him."

Tiffany said, "I don't know his name, but I saw him and another man shoot someone in front of Salvatore's a little while ago." She drew a deep breath. "Mitchell Peters was the man they shot. I'm glad you're all right, Maddie," Tiffany said.

"Is this what you meant by the senator was in deeper than I knew?"

Tiffany nodded. "We were all in deeper than we knew," she said.

The officer looked at Maddie in recognition. He pointed. "Didn't I see you on the news recently?"

Maddie nodded wearily, wondering if the officer would take her to jail along with the unconscious man. "I'm Maddie McPherson."

"You probably haven't heard the news about your boss," the police officer said to Maddie.

"Ex-boss," said Maddie.

'He's dead," the policeman said.

"Dead!" Maddie said. This day kept getting worse and worse.

"I heard a call over the radio earlier. I'm sorry to be the one to give you the bad news."

Jay pulled out his press pass. "I'm with the Washington Times. What happened to him?"

"It looks like he was murdered," the officer said.

"Murdered? Well, I didn't do it!" Maddie said hastily.

"His murderer was found with him. They were both dead," the officer said matter-of-factly.

"How horrible! Was it a robbery?" Maddie asked.

"I didn't hear what the motive was yet," replied the officer.

"This must all be related," Jay said to Maddie. "It's too big of a coincidence that there were two attacks on people who knew each other on the same night.

"Three," said Tiffany, "Mitch Peters. He was shot, although I'm sure the bullet was meant for me."

"Right, three including that Peters fellow. This guy was probably sent after the car missed Maddie," Jay said.

"Well, thanks to you, Jay, he didn't succeed," said Maddie and hugged him.

"I think you helped out quite a bit, hitting him with that flashlight and pushing him down the stairs," Jay grinned.

"Oh, I didn't push him down the stairs; he slipped on my smelly shoes and Tiffany pulled him down the stairs."

The policeman was writing it all down.

"Are you putting in the part about my shoes?" asked Maddie. "Because I stepped in something while Jay and I were wandering around in the dark looking for tainted meat that had some type of ground-up sleeping pills in it. My dog is at the vet right now because he ate that meat. It almost killed him. When we went inside, we were attacked."

"He must have planned to get your dog out of the way by putting him to sleep," said the officer. He kept writing.

"Yes, well, Franky, that's my dog, was almost put into a permanent sleep. Same for the cat next door. We can show you where the rest of the meat is."

"We'll have to collect it as evidence." There were more sirens in the distance. "The assailant probably planned on only one of you coming home. It's a good thing you were both there. You seem to work well together."

Jay put his arms around her. "And the rest is history."

After answering the officer's questions, Tiffany headed for her car. She slumped in the seat, exhausted. Where to drive to? She shook her head. Such a simple question, but she had no idea. Not her apartment ever again. She rested her weary head on the steering wheel. She still needed to get her cat from Kate.

The seductiveness had drained from the hot air balloon of power. It hadn't floated gently down either; it crash-landed, and it took Tiffany with it. Was it worth the lies, the deceptions, the bribes? For what? Power, money, prestige? She ended up with nothing. Nothing but death.

And now where could she go? She heard Mitch's voice in her head, "In Tekoa, you're always welcome."

But could she return to Tekoa? Would she be welcome with everyone knowing she was responsible for the death of the town's favorite son? Her parents would be put in danger, too. What about Mitch's parents? Could she face them? Would they ever forgiver her? Could she forgive herself?

Her cell phone rang. She looked at the readout. It was Mitch! He was alive after all! Never trust a thug when he tells you someone is dead. She was almost laughing as she said his name, "Mitch?"

"No, ma'am, my name is Henry Landers. I'm a paramedic. I'm with the team called out though for Mitch Peters."

Tiffany's heart sank. It wasn't Mitch. It was medical personnel looking for next of kin. She swallowed.

"I'm just his ex-girlfriend. His parents' numbers should be on his phone... and his sister's..." Tiffany pictured Ashley as she'd last seen her as a young teenager. Another person whose life she'd ruined.

"Tiff?"

Tiffany could barely hear the whisper of her

name.

"Mitch? Mitch is that you?"

"Tiffany, this is Henry again. We are en route to Sibley Memorial Hospital. Mitch would like you to meet him there."

"He's not dead?"

"No, ma'am, but he does need attention right away. He wouldn't let me put an oxygen mask on him until he heard your voice."

Tiffany laughed. "I'll be there as soon as I can," she said.

"One more thing. This is kind of odd. He wants to know if this counts as the train reaching the station?"

"Does it ever!" Tiffany smiled.

Maddie looked around at the chaos around her and longed for the comfort of her furry pal. "What time is it? Maybe we could pick up Franky, now. Lately, every time I've left him, I could tell he was lonely, even before tonight at the vet," Maddie said.

"Well, he's left alone all day. Maybe Franky needs another dog around to keep him company," Jay said.

"A puppy? I don't think..."

Jay interrupted, "I was thinking of Riley."

Maddie looked doubtful. "You want to give me your dog? I'm sure he's a great dog, but Franky was kind of afraid of him and ..."

Jay interrupted again, "Okay, I'm botching this." He got down on one knee. "This is kind of spontaneous, so I don't have a ring..."

"Yes!" Maddie exclaimed and grabbed him in a hug and kissed him. They both fell over in the grass.

"I didn't ask you yet," Jay managed through the kiss.

"I could tell where you were going with it." Maddie backed off from the kiss. "Uh oh."

"Mad, don't say you're bad for my career. I love you, and I want to marry you."

"No, it's not that. I think we fell in something."

A few days later, when Maddie was able to put her phone back together, she received this text message from Dalton Stanfield posthumously:

UR in danger. Not long 2 live. Told lies about u. D Washburn ordered my killing 4 plans 2 blackmail president. Sorry 4 using u as bait 4 a trap. Plz 4giv

Made in the USA
Columbia, SC
05 October 2021